THE Wonder OF YOU

*Falling down the rabbit hole's
never been such a rush.*

HARPER KINCAID

Dedicated to my husband, David,
I am beyond grateful and ecstatic I get to share my life with you.

You are my Wonderland.

One

"Little Alice fell
d
o
w
n
the hOle,
bumped her head
and bruised her soul"
~Lewis Carroll, *Alice in Wonderland*

Alice

"GREAT REAR VIEW, princess, but put some hustle in it. I need this cab."

I didn't even bother looking behind me because I was already frazzled enough, scrambling to scoop the last of my belongings off the cab floor and into the cardboard box I'd swiped from a liquor store.

Moments like these made me miss back home: ironic because when I was there I couldn't get out of that Southern flytrap fast enough.

"You going to keep wiggling those sweet cheeks for me or finish up already? I don't have all day."

"Hey. Newsflash, jackass: I am *not* your personal bachelor party and this is not *your* cab. So feel free to throw that white male privilege you're carrying 'round somewhere else."

"You're kidding me, right? Favors courtesy of the patriarchy don't apply during rush hour; it's survival of the fittest."

"Is that right?" I asked.

"Yeah that's right," he said. "So feel free to take that 'fight the power' *schtick* back over the bridge to the other hipsters the next time you hit Urban Outfitters."

Sigh. So much for enlightened, twenty-first century gender parity or old-fashioned chivalry. Welcome to New York City—definitely another kind of Wonderland.

My sister, with the last of my huge duffels on her shoulder, had already gotten out from the other side of the cab and was getting impatient. With him, not me.

"Is everything okay? Is this 'gentleman' bothering you?"

I heard him chuckle. Guess he caught her tone. God, I loved my sister—she never did suffer fools lightly.

I crawled backwards out of the cab, box tucked under one arm while blowing my hair out of my eyes.

"Yeah, I'm good. Don't mind him. He's grouchy and without a trace of manners, but he's harmless."

She dropped the duffels on the sidewalk, ready to thrown down.

Just in case.

"Get used to it, sis," Caroline advised, both hands in fists on her hips like Wonder Woman. "That's what happens when men think swiping right is the same as opening a door for a lady."

Even after being in the city for the last eighteen months, my sister hadn't lost a fraction of her Southern belle ways and was still a stickler for civility. I blamed it on the day job—she helped run an etiquette school, teaching manners and social graces to the graceless.

"Hey, Daisy Mae, time to wrap up the Ya Ya Sisterhood meet and greet and move it along."

Of course, some people were hopeless cases from the get-go.

I turned around, ready to slap the spit out of his head, but instead I almost smacked myself face first into a wall of muscle. I craned my head up until I finally met his gaze.

I think I gasped. In fact, I know I did because he had the nerve to wink at me, with these lush green eyes rimmed in gold, flashing something I couldn't read.

Okay, so he was gorgeous and totally my type, especially with his silky black hair kept long in the front and short on the sides. The beard was even better: dark, rugged and full.

He wasn't like the other men I had encountered so far—metrosexuals with more hair product than sense. And dear Lord, he was tall and built like a linebacker. Even with my boots on, I only came up to the middle of his chest.

But one look and I knew he was arrogant. He had already proven as much with his rudeness. Caroline was motioning me to get a move on, but for some reason I couldn't yet. I gave her the eyes, which she knew meant I'd meet her upstairs.

"I get you're in a rush and all, but there was no need for you to get ugly about it."

His brows shot straight up. "Get ugly?"

I rolled my eyes. "It means being rude."

That explanation earned me a crooked smile this time.

"Also, it's impolite to mock where someone is from," I went on.

The bastard was still amused, that luscious mouth of his forming another lopsided grin. "And how did I manage to do that, sweet cheeks?"

I narrowed my eyes into slits. "Do *not* call me sweet cheeks."

"Calling you sweet cheeks makes you blush, and I've gotta admit, I can't remember the last time I made a woman blush. I like it. Suits you, Daisy Mae."

I felt my nipples pebble under my dress. Damn it—why did my body only come

to life around arrogant assholes? Unfortunately, I knew why. I studied stuff like this for a living. Nevertheless, I dug my nails into my palms. Maybe some homemade aversion therapy would stop every nerve in my being from reacting to him.

I lifted my chin. "You're also making the stereotypical assumption that everyone from the South has two first names. Not true—and it only makes you look like an ignorant Yankee saying so."

"Duly noted," he said, not even trying to hide the humor in his voice—a voice that was deep and sonorous. He took a small step closer.

"You know, you could clear up this horrible stereotype I've got going by telling me your name."

I scoffed, all while being thrilled he wanted to know me, even if it was probably just to get me into bed. I may have been drawn to beautiful, arrogant men, but at least I knew it. There was just no way I was going to let *him* know it.

"I don't give out my personal information to men who learned their manners courtesy of Tinder." That comment only earned me an even bigger face-splitting grin. *Smiling looks real good on him,* I thought. *Damn.*

"And just because I'm from the South doesn't make me stupid, you know."

I wasn't going down without a fight.

"Never thought you were dumb for one second, Daisy Mae."

He was teasing me—and enjoying it way too much, and if I was honest with myself, so was I. For the record, I wasn't admitting my enjoyment to myself just yet. No way.

"You're doing it again," I said.

"Doing *what,* exactly?"

He totally knew what he was doing.

"You *know,*" I said. "Using that infuriating stereotypical name, just to get my panties in a wad."

His eyes heated, his gaze moving back and forth between my eyes and my mouth. "Do yourself a favor, sweet cheeks," he said. "You're in New York, not Dixie Chicks Hollow. Don't talk about your panties with strangers."

"Fine," I spat out. "Stop calling me 'Daisy Mae.'"

"I'm happy to put the whole 'Daisy Mae' debacle to bed," he said. "Just give me a better name for my mouth to play with."

"I don't think so, City."

He was close enough now for me to catch a hint of his scent: Indian sandalwood and fresh linens, with a dash of Tahitian vanilla underneath (Don't judge. I used to work at the cologne counter at the mall back home). I took a step back, banging my behind into the open cab door.

"Hey, watch it, lady! Are you in or out?" the driver yelled.

That was enough to break the spell. "Don't get your knickers in a knot. I'm out of here," I said back to him.

I stepped out of the way, but tall, dark, and unfortunately magnificent put his hand on my upper arm, giving it a quick squeeze. My heart became a butterfly and fluttered its wings inside my chest.

"Just so you know, if I wasn't running late for a meeting, I wouldn't have been rushing you and your sister off."

My mind often worked like a Pinterest board, with pictures and words popping in and out. I blamed it on too many late nights scrolling through the app's awesomeness. This time, it was a quote from Maya Angelou:

The first time someone shows you who they are, believe them.

And just like that, the butterflies stopped fluttering.

"Is that right?"

"Yeah, that's right." He studied my face, his brows knitting together. "What?"

I shrugged my shoulders and moved out of his hold. "I think being rude and pushing people out of your way is probably who you are—either that, or it's who you've become. One's true character reveals itself when things aren't convenient."

City stilled, his mouth gaped, and he looked like he was about to say something, but I wasn't sticking around long enough to hear him out. I was a New Yorker in training now. That meant I didn't have to 'bless his heart,' or 'pray for' him or anyone I didn't want to anymore. I said goodbye to all that the day I drove through Lincoln Tunnel.

I may have fallen down the rabbit hole, but I didn't fall off the turnip truck. Guys like City always got what they wanted. And this time, he wasn't going to get me.

Two

"It's no use going back to yesterday,
because I was a different person then."
~Lewis Carroll, *Alice in Wonderland*

Dare

"... *BEING RUDE, PUSHING people out of your way, is probably who you are—either that or who you've become.*"

I couldn't remember the last time someone called me on my shit. Well, that's not entirely true. Ingrid certainly laid me out, almost daily, but she was also a woman who had not one shred of interest in my cock or my wallet.

The ones who did never put me in my place.

The kicker was, instead of being pissed, I was intrigued. Her words were running through my damn mind on a continuous loop.

Fuck, why didn't I get her name?

I was finally in the cab, on my way to somewhere I didn't want to go. I stretched my legs out, until my foot hit something soft and bulky. I leaned over to discover an oversized leather purse, partially wedged under the passenger seat.

Two scenarios crashed through my brain at the exact same time: (1) It's a bomb and this was how I was going to bite it, or (2) the purse belongs to either Ms. Dixie or her sister.

My pulse quickened, just from the hope the bag belonged to the girl whose bee-stung, pink mouth was now playing the starring role in my latest fantasies. If she was like most women, she would have a ridiculous amount of crap in this bag—and I was sure as shit hoping she did so I could find out more about her.

Her name would be the perfect start.

I pulled on the end of my beard, thinking how much I valued my privacy. I would understand if she was the same, which meant I should just look for her ID and hand it off to Ingrid. Let her handle the rest.

But that would mean I would never know much about her. I'd be no better off than I am now—another asshole with a hard on who did nothing about it.

Nope, not gonna happen.

No way.

If this was her bag and she had been careless enough to leave it behind—in a New York City cab of all places—then I had every right to go spelunking through her possessions.

"Fuck it," I mumbled to myself, and I hoisted the bag onto my lap.

I released the zipper and peered inside.

Oh, there was a bomb in there all right, but it wasn't the kind I was expecting. Almost hidden, I spotted a hot pink, crushed velvet, drawstring bag, with a logo I'd recognize anywhere: one of New York's most popular sex novelty stores.

Which meant anything—and I mean *anything*—could be inside her little pink bag of tricks, assuming it belonged to my Southern girl.

Until I knew exactly who owned this purse, I wasn't going to loosen that drawstring. Rummaging through this woman's bag was a task that would require proper attention—one I planned on giving one hundred percent of my focus. I took out my phone and made a call.

"Hey, it's me. Yeah, postpone my meeting and reschedule for this evening. In fact, clear the rest of my day."

"Are you sure?" Ingrid asked.

"They want me. I don't need them," I reminded her. "Just say I secured a reservation for that restaurant everyone keeps talking about . . . Christ, I can't remember the name."

"You don't mean *Protzig*, do you?"

"Yeah, that's the one. I know for a fact they've been trying to get in there for months now, with no luck. Then call over there and make the res."

"Dude, that's the most in-demand restaurant in the city right now."

"Well then, I guess you've been rewarded with your first challenge of the day," I said.

"That's quite the inspirational speech, chief. Remind me to include it in the montage for your memorial service someday."

Being rude, pushing people out of your way, is probably who you are—either that or who you've become.

I couldn't get that brunette spitfire out of my head. She was right. I *had* turned into a self-centered prick. In fairness, I was never the 'nice' guy. I had almost zero tolerance for bullshit and I wanted everything to happen yesterday, but that came with my New York birth certificate.

I expelled a harsh breath. "If anyone can do it, you can, Ingrid. I honestly don't know what I would do without you. You're the shit."

There was a long pause. "Hey, you still there?" I asked.

"That's the first time, in almost a year, you've given me a compliment."

Shit, had it been a year already? I really was an asshole.

"Don't worry about it. I've got this," she added.

I thanked her and hung up, then gave the cabbie the address for the studio.

There were a million possessions to explore, but first I needed to ensure it all belonged to the right woman. I grabbed the phone inside the bag and hit the home button, but unfortunately, it was password protected.

"Smart girl," I murmured. Fortunately though, her screensaver had a photo of her and three other women with their arms around each other, clearly in the middle of sharing something hilarious because all of them were laughing. I felt an unexpected stab of jealousy. I couldn't remember the last time I had that good a time, really letting it all hang out.

Unfortunately, her sister was also in the picture, so there was no way to know which one owned the phone. I tossed it back and started searching. There was some make up, a small bottle of hand sanitizer, a lot of Uniball pens and a couple boxes of those nuclear-strength ginger-flavored mints.

I finally found her wallet, and there it was: a school ID with her photo.
Alice Elizabeth Leighton
Doctoral Candidate, Clinical Psychology / Human Sexuality Studies
Hudson University
Student # 837462
Jackpot, it's her.

And holy shit, she studied *sex*. I didn't want to sound like some nineteen-year-old frat boy, but fuck, that was hot. I couldn't help but feel a rush of blood leave my brain and rush straight to my dick, with the fantasy of her as the naughty professor in a short-as-hell plaid skirt and a white, button-down top, keeping me after school to have her way with me.

Only problem with my fantasy is that the girl in real life wanted nothing to do with me. She wouldn't even give me her name. But there had been heat between us, until she figured out I was a selfish asshole and blew me off.

Alice had my number in less than five minutes.

She had balls for telling me off, and self-respect for walking away. And for the first time in a really long time, I wanted to prove I was worth someone's time, versus what I usually did—try to make a woman prove she was worth mine.

Guess I'm going to have to work a little to get in there.

This will be good for me, I thought. When was the last time I actually had to exert any real effort to get a woman into bed? Although, after what happened, I hadn't had anyone in my bed for over a year. I hadn't seen the point and, besides, it had always come easy.

Too easy.

There she was in her ID photo, the perfect picture of that Cheshire grin in the palm of my hand. She had her glossy dark, bourbon-colored hair twisted into one of those messy buns on top of her head, with glasses perched on the tip of her nose. The only thing missing was a pencil behind her ear. She was every bit the graduate student, intellectual and adorable all at once.

Now that I was sure this monstrosity of a purse was hers, I was going to enjoy exploring the shit out of it and I had no intention of playing fair.

Fuck that.

I wanted this woman.

She had a couple of concrete blocks posing as textbooks in there. The first one was *Obeying the Master: Evolution of Human Sexuality in the Kink Community*. Man, that's a hot title. But after thumbing through a few pages, I laughed to myself, because leave it to a bunch of tight-assed academics to make a topic like kinky sex read like stereo instructions.

The other one wasn't any more interesting. Pity. I was always up for learning something new.

She had a lined, spiral notebook in there too, with a shit-ton of sex info, citing trends and statistics in the U.S. and worldwide, along with some interesting commentary of her own. Alice may be a good lil' grad student, but she was no bloodless academic. Just looking through the margins, I could tell she had a fire in her belly that was anything but textbook.

"Hey buddy, ride's over," the cabbie said over his shoulder.

"Oh right," I glanced at the meter and gave the guy a fifty. "Keep the change."

The cabbie kept thanking me, which always made me uncomfortable, so I pushed out fast. I shoved the notebook back in and cradled the bag under my arm. I knew I was demonstrating a level of weirdness, even for me, but I didn't want anyone even *looking* at her bag. I wanted to be the only one who got the chance to explore what was inside Alice's head.

Being raised by a single mom, I knew a woman's purse wasn't just someplace to keep her shit together. It was a small, portable caravan of her life with everything she held important, like a tangible, tactile diary.

Of course, I made a living, a really good one, out of finding meaning in ordinary objects, of taking the discarded and transforming them into something new. So there was a strong possibility I was building up this impromptu scavenger hunt, and this woman, into way more than I should. She sure as hell was beautiful, and having a backbone made her even more captivating, especially when I thought about . . . well, the shit I tried not thinking about anymore.

Because thinking about what happened has never made the present any better and I haven't found anything close to an answer. Maybe not getting an answer to the countless pleas to any higher power that would listen was the universe's way of telling me I didn't deserve a reprieve—getting no answer was my punishment for playing God.

I shook my head, physically trying to rid myself of that train wreck. For now, I wanted to shut myself off from the world and get to know this woman.

As soon as I walked into the studio, I spotted Ingrid standing over one of her canvases, placed on the floor in front of her. Rail thin, she was wearing her usual uniform of jean shorts over ripped black tights, swimming in an oversized sweatshirt, with her Doc Martens and a beanie covering her electric blue hair.

"Everything taken care of?" I saddled up next to her, studying her progress.

"Yeah, total cake," she answered without losing focus on her painting. "Maybe someday it'll sink in that your name is like a Wonka golden ticket."

"Still?

She met my gaze, cocking one brow straight up like a super villain. "Hells yeah. In fact," she turned, reaching over to her desk, grabbing a message slip, "here's another one for your collage. It's a beauty."

Confirmed dinner for three, 8:30pm. Make sure to ask for Tiffany. She's the VIP liaison. Her personal cell is 917.555.0439 if you need her before or after your reservation.

She also asked if you were 'involved' and what you liked in a woman.

PS: I should get a raise for having to deal with this shit.

PPS: The feminist revolution wept today. It was a long, ugly cry.

I let out a sound between a laugh and a bark.

"How did you answer this time?"

Being my assistant for so long, she was asked on a consistent basis if we were together or whom else I may be fucking. In the beginning she'd just roll her eyes, but once my career took off, she had a list of retorts at the ready.

She shrugged her shoulders. "I went for truth this time. I told her I was a gold star, Chapstick lesbian who'd rock her world more than *you* ever could. That seemed to shut her up."

I put out my fist, which she bumped back without even having to look up from her work.

"*Nice,*" I said, handing the slip back. "Just mark out the contact info and put it with the others."

"Will do," she said as she shoved it into her pocket. "Got enough yet?"

"Probably, but it's always good to have extras."

I was currently working on an art piece partially made out of all the slips of paper given to me since I'd become famous. Business cards, torn matchbook covers with phone numbers scrawled inside . . . all had various come-ons and requests. I had quite a collection, enough to make a three dimensional, mixed media sculpture depicting a battle between the gods Narcissus and Nemesis, my own postmodern reinterpretation of the Greek myth.

"Should I ask why you're cradling a woman's purse like it's your 'precious?'"

I couldn't help but smile to myself, knowing she couldn't go a day without at least one Lord of the Rings or CS Lewis reference—some of the few decent residuals emanating from her strict, religious upbringing. I met her inquisitive gaze. "Nothing for you to worry about."

"'Mmhmm." She wasn't buying it, but I wasn't surprised; Ingrid had a built-in bullshit detector. Guess her time living on the streets honed that skill. I tried not to think about the way I found her because it made me want to punch things, mainly her parents.

"I'm going up," I told her. "So, no calls, no interruptions. Got it?"

She gave a smart-assed salute. "Aye aye, captain. Enjoy getting in touch with your feminine side."

I offered her the bird as my response, although she knew me well enough by now to know it didn't have any real ire behind it.

Moving through the studio never got old, especially having this amount of square footage in the city. While everyone else was running from lower Manhattan after 9–11, I knew I could take that chunk of change I'd gotten from my father-slash-sperm donor and actually afford a decent-sized, live/work space. My building used to be, of all things, an international bank with offices above. Now, the first three floors were studio space and everything above that was apartments I rented out.

The top floor was all mine though. My sanctuary. And that's where I was headed now.

I had gutted the top floor myself; keeping the industrial feel and making sure it was designed with as little clutter as possible. Every time I came home, I'd see my city through the floor-to-ceiling windows, taking in the surrounding skyline that stretched to the stars—and I felt as close to settled and peaceful as I ever have.

I sank into the corner of my L-shaped suede sectional, cracked all my knuckles at once and settled in. Just as I'd expected, there was a whole world in her bag.

I went back to her lined notebook because, even though most of what was inside appeared to be dull-as-shit lecture notes, she did have some cool doodles, random thoughts and quotes peppered along the margins.

Just thumbing through each page, I could imagine her sitting in class with those sexy librarian glasses on and her hair in a knot on the top of her head, chewing on the end of her pen, half listening to some fossil droning on.

Man, did she know all these quotes off the top of her head or did she write them down as she heard them? Some were deep, but others were funny as hell:

You cannot make everybody happy.
You are not a taco.

Group projects help me understand
Why Batman works alone

I will never
Apologize for being me.
You should apologize for asking me to be
Anything else.

In my defense,
The moon was full and I was left
Unsupervised.

I felt like I was getting a cheat sheet on everything Alice. I may not have known the particulars, but I certainly could surmise their effects. I was getting to know her in a way I had not earned.

Crawl inside
This body,
Find me
Where I am most ruined
Love me there.
~Rune Lazuli

That last one slayed me, sucker punching me right in the gut. *No way. I'll never let anyone get under my skin like that again.*

Not again.

Never again.

The only thing left that I hadn't violated, was that hot pink, drawstring bag. I knew I should have left it alone, that once I looked inside, I wouldn't be able to stop thinking about how she used it on herself.

"Fuck it," I mumbled, untying the perfect bow she had made and loosened the strings' hold. Sure enough, inside was a bottle of lube and a vibrator. I sucked in a harsh breath as my cock swelled, straining against my zipper.

I couldn't help but imagine her using that toy while I watched, spreading those porcelain white legs wide apart for me so I could admire her delectable, hot pink center. Alice may have been little, doll-like even, with those big blue eyes, but she was no girl. She was a woman—one who owned her sexual needs and desires. Her carrying around her vibrator was the hottest fucking thing I'd ever discovered, like she kept it close in case she had an 'emergency' and needed to get off ASAP.

I wanted to know more about this woman, especially how she tasted and sounded when she let it all go. That meant, for the first time in a long while, I was going to do the chasing.

Three

"I knew who I WAS when I got up this morning, but I
think I must have been changed several times since then."
~Lewis Carroll, *Alice in Wonderland*

Alice

"I CANNOT BELIEVE I did that. In the history of my entire life, I have
never, *ever* done something so, so . . ." I was so worked up I couldn't even
finish my sentence.

"Alice, you're twenty-five years old and have been stuck in the same
state your whole life until a month ago. Your entire life hasn't happened
yet," Caroline said. She may have thought I was overreacting, but that
didn't stop my sister from helping me search through her apartment. I
knew it was no use. My purse wasn't here—and it wasn't back at the room
I had temporarily rented until one of my sister's roommates had moved
out. I had called, but I knew I was wasting my time.

A shock of white blond hair poked through my doorway, attached
to a girl with pale grey eyes rapidly blinking.

"Alice, what's wrong? You look like you lost your pet puppy or something."

It was Lulu, one of the remaining roommates in the place I now shared with my sister in Chelsea. They had a two-and-a-half bedroom—yeah I know, don't ask, 'cuz only in New York would a misshapen nook count as a half bedroom. It was still a space Lulu and Caroline had gotten some rent money for, so them, offering it to me free of charge was huge. My program offered university housing at a reduced rate for doctoral students, but it was still ridiculous. I was devoting to studying sexuality, but I didn't want to work a pole in order to finance it.

Of course, I had offered to pay something for the space, which was only big enough for a twin and a storage locker, but both girls insisted they were good as long as I kept their place neat and in groceries. I knew it was just my sister's way of letting me save face. She didn't need me for neatness; she was totally OCD about her apartment. Everything always had its place.

Everything except my bag, which was still missing.

"I lost my purse," I said, feeling my throat getting all tight. "This guy, this total jerk, who needed a cab got me all flustered. I think I left it in there."

Lulu was fidgeting with her hands while biting the corner of her lip, acting like a skittish, scared-of-its-own-shadow little rabbit. When I had first met her, I thought she was on something because, well, no *way* was someone that naturally high-strung and anxious, but I soon realized that was how Lulu got when she felt out of control.

"This is my fault. I should've called into work and asked for the morning off so I could've helped you two today."

"Me being empty-headed has not one thing to do with you, honey," I tried to console her. "Don't take that on, 'kay?"

She shrugged, tucking both hands inside her jean pockets and letting out a slow breath, one of the techniques she told me she had learned in therapy.

That's another thing I've learned since coming to New York: you couldn't swing a dead cat without hitting either a therapist or someone going to therapy.

I knew Lulu never took more than three seconds to consider what she was going to wear on any given day, but I still appreciated the chuckle I got reading her T-shirt: Computer engineers know it's not the length of the vector that counts but how you apply the force.

Yeah, she was a total nerd. She wasn't just smart, Lulu was like Mensa-level, thank sweet Jesus she's hasn't succumbed to the dark side, brilliant. Oh, and she was crazy-beautiful too.

I'd almost consider rear-ending a van full of nuns for bone structure like hers. The only thing she lacked was sense; the woman was living proof common sense wasn't so common after all.

"Well, did you have anything important in it?"

That stopped me cold. Dear Lord, for someone who was a certifiable genius, she could be scarily clueless sometimes.

"You're kidding me, right? You *do* realize most women don't walk around with their keys and a billfold on a lanyard like a cowbell around their neck, like you do."

My bad mood had no effect on her. She shrugged her shoulders again. "Well, maybe you should. It's really convenient. What else do you need besides keys, a credit card, ID, and lip balm?"

"It wasn't just my bag, it was my portable lifeline. Besides my wallet and make-up, I had my class notes, a couple of textbooks worth more than my kidneys, not to mention Eduardo."

"Who's Eduardo?" Caroline asked as she walked into the 'room.'

"That's the name of her vibrator," Lulu clarified for her.

That comment earned me a judgey look. "So let me see if I've got this right: My sister—who's already studying to be a sex therapist—not only *names* her vibrator but also takes 'him' wherever she goes?"

"It's highly probable that other women in New York do the same," Lulu said. "Fifty three percent of the population of New York is female. That's a little over four-and-a-half million women. Recent statistics show that one in three women owns a vibrator. So it's totally feasible that, out of one point three million—"

"Thank *you*, Dr. Kinsey. That'll do," my sister interrupted, all while giving me the stink-eye. "And don't encourage her. Alice is already a unique enough creation."

"Don't look at me like I'm touched in the head or something," I said.

Both her hands were up, palms out. "Absolutely not. It's totally normal for someone to carry their sex toys around with them—in their *pocketbook*."

"First of all, it's a bag. No one's used the word 'pocketbook' since 1955. And second of all, I usually don't carry it around, but even if I did, there'd be nothing wrong with it. I just shoved it in there when I was packing all my stuff is all."

Just then, Rayna—friend and neighbor, who lived in the penthouse of our building—walked in, surveying the unholy mess I had made in my attempt to find my bag.

"Hey, you know your front door was wide open. Everything okay?"

My sister crossed her arms in front of her chest. "Alice, I know you've only been in the city for only a short time, but you have *got* to remember you're not in Devil's Peak anymore."

I could feel my face and neck turn red. "You're right, you're right. I'm really sorry."

"What's going on?" Rayna asked while leaning her curvy hip against the doorjamb.

I recounted the story of my carelessness yet again.

"Well, if you can remember the name of the cab company, I'll call them for you."

I met Rayna's gaze. "Thanks, that would be great, but let's face it: this is New York. It's as good as gone."

"True, but I'll give it a try," she said as she whipped out her phone and dialed the number of the cab company I gave her. She walked into the other room so she could hear. In the meantime, Lulu was also standing by the doorway, looking like she didn't know whether she was coming or going. That's when I remembered.

"Hey, I know you're meeting with Beck soon. No need to stick around here. It'll be okay."

Beck was *the* Beckett MacMillan—as in the founder of MacMillan Technologies—and he was considering backing some of Lulu's inventions. Turns out he was just as much of an obsessed gadget geek as she was, and he obviously recognized genius when he found it.

"If you're sure . . ." she hedged. "You know I hate being late. It's an important date."

"Go," I insisted. "And use that gloss I got you. It'll plump your lips and make them even more luscious than they already are."

She shook her head. "Thanks, but I'm sticking to my Coca Cola lip balm. The scent of high fructose corn syrup soothes me."

"Alright nerd girl, hop along then." I grinned. "Good luck. Be safe."

"Will do!" she waved while skipping down the hall and out the front door. At least *she* remembered to close it behind her.

Rayna suppressed a grin, shaking her head. "She's gone over him, isn't she?"

I did a combo laugh-snort. "What gave it away?"

Her expression grew somber. "Yeah, well listen, the cab company contacted the driver. He checked the cab, but your purse wasn't in there."

"Yeah, it's already been hours. I really appreciate you trying though." I rested my head in the palms of my hands, elbows on my knees.

"Lo siento, *chiquita*," Rayna said. "I've gotta go," she turned her attention to my sister. "Lock the door behind me."

Caroline got up to follow her, answering her cell phone along the way. Meanwhile, I grabbed some paper and tried to list all the credit cards and other personal information that could've been in my lost wallet.

It didn't take long.

I had two credit cards (one maxed out), my school ID and my North Carolina-issued driver's license, which I hadn't had a chance to change over yet. Oh, and an almost full punch card from Red Cat Burger. What's sad is I was more upset about losing the card for a free burger than the cards.

"Um, Alls?" my sister was back, holding the phone to her ear with her hand over the mouthpiece. I've told her a dozen times about a revolutionary feature called the mute button, but it just doesn't stick.

"What's up, buttercup?"

"There's some guy calling for you on *my* cell, saying he needs to speak with you directly."

My brows knitted, until I remembered. "I put you down as my emergency contact at school. Maybe someone turned in my bag and figured you're the way to let me know?"

"Or maybe it's that freaktard professor of yours."

Even though I was taking five classes this term, I already knew she meant Professor Bails.

"Don't start now," I told her. "He's a huge deal. I'm lucky he took a first year into his seminar."

"Whatever, if you ask me, that man's completely under the weather upstairs," she said, tapping her finger to her temple. "Don't let him piss all over you and convince you it's raining, okay?"

"Fine, fine, just give me the phone already," I snatched her cell out of her hand. "You've got Alice here."

I heard a low-throttle, sexy chuckle on the other end of the line. I knew that sounds weird—a 'sexy' chuckle—but the stranger on the other end of the line had it.

Definitely not Professor Bails. He had more of a death-rattle smoker's cough.

"Hello? Who's this?"

"I'm the guy who found your bag."

A rush of relief flooded my body and I felt all the tension drain right out of me. "Oh thank God! I've been trying to figure out what I was going to do without it."

"Yeah, I bet. You carry a lot of crap with you."

My eyes turned to slits. Not that he could tell, but still. "My stuff is *not* crap."

I heard him laugh again and that's when it hit me—I was talking to the guy who kicked me out of my cab. The one with the lumberjack beard and delicious man scent.

Hey, don't judge. That's totally a thing.

"My theory is you subconsciously left your bag behind because it was too much of a burden. It was your mind's way of doing some much needed housekeeping."

"Is that right?"

"That's right." He sounded so sure of himself.

Arrogant prick.

"Are you a therapist of some kind?" I asked.

"Nope," he said with a smile in his voice. "But that doesn't mean I'm wrong. I'm just giving it to you straight."

Unbelievable. "Well, thank you kindly for bestowing your gifts upon me. You know, I bet you think the sun comes up every morning just to hear you crow."

He let out a laugh, not the kind that mocked you, but a rich and soulful one, the type that filled up empty spaces you didn't know you had. I pushed the feeling aside.

I shouldn't have asked the next question, but I couldn't help myself. "Uh . . . how much did you ransack through my personal belongings?"

Silence. Heavy, weighted silence hung in the air for several seconds. "Well, I'll tell you . . . usually I would have just tossed it on my assistant's desk and had her contact you. But once I saw what you had in that velvet pouch, I had to talk to you myself."

He was talking about my battery-operated-boyfriend (B.O.B.), Eduardo.

"I bet you did," I huffed. "Alright, so you found my vibrator. Here's a twenty-first century newsflash: women own sex toys. We use them and we make no apologies for it. So if you're expecting me to get all discomfited because you discovered I'm a wholly evolved, sexual being, you're going to be disappointed."

"Discomfited?"

"Embarrassed," I clarified.

"I know what discomfited means," he answered. "I just don't think I've ever heard someone use it in casual conversation before."

"Well, then you need to reach beyond your raisin'," I said. "Aim higher."

"I should've assumed a woman pursuing her doctorate degree in human sexuality studies wasn't going to get all tongue tied over a rocket tucked in the side pocket."

"Wow, you really plundered through every nook and cranny, didn't you there?"

"Now, don't get in a snit. I really was just searching for a way to get in touch with you. Your driver license is still from below the Mason Dixon line. Good thing I found your school ID."

"Mmhmm," I said, unconvinced. "How did you get my sister's cell number? Why didn't you just contact the university and have them handle it?"

"My assistant's a bloodhound and can find anyone. Once I found your name, the rest was easy. And I wasn't going to leave your stuff with a stranger at your school."

"So why am I talking to *you* and not your assistant?"

That question was met with silence on the other end for several beats.

"Hello?"

"I think you know the answer to that, Alice."

An electric thrill ran through me, especially hearing him say my name.

"You know, City, I never got your name earlier."

"Ah, so you recognize my voice?" He seemed pleased, which gave me a jolt of happy. Gawd, I was such a girl sometimes. Why should I care what he thinks?

"Dare," he said.

"What dare? What are you talking about?"

"No, I mean my name is Dare."

"*Dare*? Your name is *Dare*? What the heck, did you parents lose a bet or something?"

Caroline started giggling but had enough manners to cover her mouth while she was doing it. Frankly, until she made a sound, I had forgotten she was even in the room with me.

"Uh no, far from it," he reassured me, surprisingly not offended at all by my snide remark. "It's an old family name."

"Uh-huh," I said, tasting something sour in my mouth. The only people who ever used family names for their progeny came from money. "So, you're one of *those*."

"One of those *what*, Ms. Leighton? Enlighten me."

I was being incredibly rude, but nothing I said seemed to rattle him. If anything, he seemed to be getting off on it. The calmer he was, the more he was pushing my buttons.

"You're high cotton," I mumbled under my breath. Caroline glanced up, meeting my gaze as she shook her head, which totally said it all: if neither of us ever dealt with another entitled douche-a-saurus for the rest of our days, it still would be a day too soon.

"Do you always make a shit-ton of assumptions about people before you've even had a chance to get to know them?"

I sighed into the phone. "I'd like to say I don't, but now that you bring it up, I'm thinking I do, like all the time. I should work on that."

"Hold back the reins now," he teased, imitating my accent, or at least trying to. "Is that an apology I'm hearing? Am I hallucinating right now?"

"Alright, alright, I deserve that," I said. "Let's move it along now."

"Well, why don't we meet so you can see if your hunch about me is right? And bonus, you'll get your precious cargo back."

Oh dear Lord, I had forgotten all about my bag. Where was my head at?

I knew exactly where it was at: wondering if that beard of his felt as deliciously rough between my legs as his voice did between my ears.

Gawd!

I needed to cut this off at the knees. Now.

"Okay, so we're both busy people. Tell me where you work and I'll pick up my bag from your assistant."

"I've got a better idea," he countered. "Why don't you give me your address and I'll bring it to you?"

"If you got my sister's cell number, then I'm thinking you know where I live already."

He didn't answer, which was answer enough.

"Well, thank you for not just showing up and scaring the stuffing out of me."

That one earned me another chuckle. "Alright, so why don't you come pick it up at my apartment?"

"Uh no—and if any woman agreed to that it means her elevator doesn't go all the way to the top floor, if you understand my meaning."

"I know what it means, Dixie. I'm just wondering how many Southern colloquialisms I'm going to be on the receiving end of in one conversation."

"Well, I'd count those up for you, City, but I'm too busy with all the different nicknames you've got rolling off your tongue to be of any real help."

If I wasn't mistaken, I heard a low moan. "Alright, come to my studio instead. I've got people around, so you'll be safe."

"City, did you forget? You have my wallet."

"Then, I'll send a car for you. Ten sharp."

"That's four hours from now. What am I supposed to do until—?"

"Gotta go Dixie."

"Gawd! Are you always this, this—?"

"Assertive? Charming? Irresistible? Why yes . . . yes, I am actually."

I emitted something between a growl and a groan.

"Oh and Alice?"

"Yes, Dare," I snapped.

"Don't even *think* of sending someone else. Because I'm not giving your bag to anyone but you."

And then, wouldn't you know it? The son-of-a-bitch hung up on me.

Four

"Would you tell me, please, which way I ought to go from here?"
"That depends a good deal on where you want to get to."
"I don't much care where–"
"Then it doesn't matter which way you go."
~Lewis Carroll, *Alice in Wonderland*

Dare

"WE'RE GOING TO this *lit* club below Houston."

"Just an FYI, we're a *really* open couple."

"Want a bump?"

That last comment from the strangers across the table from me earned them my exit. Typical star-fuckers. I had a feeling they were less interested in a commission than they claimed, but I had still taken the meeting. I knew plenty of other artists who thought I was crazy for still taking on commissioned work, because it was, almost always, a pain in the ass.

But once you've been broke, you don't squander one second of your shot to ensure you stay in the black. When I got into this, I knew I was aiming for something more elusive than a fucking unicorn sighting in Central Park—to be able to live off what I made as an artist. None of us signed a magical lifetime contract stating that people were going to continue to buy our work. The art world is a fickle mistress.

I tossed enough cash out to cover the bill and got the hell out of there. I never touched drugs and I didn't hang with those who did. I hardly drank either. I was also especially particular where I dipped my dick.

It wasn't entirely their fault for assuming what they did about me. Many years back, I did an interview. To say it was a good write up would be an understatement; my mother couldn't have written a better one. But the reporter utilized some colorful analogies, and let's just say, I'd had to fend off my share of wife swappers and cocaine cowboys ever since.

I usually didn't give a fuck. If dealing with a handful of fame whores was the price I paid for a life almost completely of my own creation, I was good with that. I understood my public image was based, in large part, on other people's fantasies of the New York art world. I considered my role like theater, a revolving performance art piece.

I walked back to the studio where I was going to meet up with Alice. It was the first Thursday of the month, which meant we were open to the public, so by the time I arrived, the place was already buzzing.

The whole ground floor was open space with whitewashed brick and exposed pipes. Ingrid kept paintings, drawings, and mixed media work on one side and photography on the other. I positioned myself off to the side, in front of a storage closet that had ascending steps. I stood at the top stair, so I could purview the whole of the crowd, hoping to catch a glimpse of her.

A labyrinth of bodies of every color and size swirled and swayed between the smatterings of support beams throughout the square footage, instinctually moving towards and away from one another in a hypnotic rhythm. There was a DJ perched in the center of the room, spinning vinyl, holding the cans around her head.

It wasn't my birthday or anything, but it sure felt like it every time we invited the outside world inside Grangeworth Gallery & Studios. I had to admit, one of my favorite things was having someone come in convinced art wasn't for them, only to have a piece of their consciousness awaken as they found something here that turned their souls inside out. Bearing witness to that was like getting a present. And I swear, I didn't even care if it was one of my works, although I'd be lying if I didn't admit I got a shot of adrenalin when it turned out something I made was the catalyst for someone to experience the world in a different way.

I stood perusing the expanse of faces and bodies, broad movements and loud sounds, enjoying a room that had always been larger than life for me. That is, until that second when I finally spotted all five feet nothing of her, so small and far away. Even with her curves, she was still a wisp of a woman. And yet, there was something about her, as if she was lit from the inside out.

Without thinking, my feet moved forward. I was caught in her magnetic field, pulled by a force stronger than my natural inclination to stand back and observe.

I was weightless, hovering in the space between before and afters. I did and did not know this woman. I had no clue what was going to happen. All I knew was that instead of being pulled into a black hole, an endless abyss I had known for way too long, I saw a sliver of light in the shape of a bourbon-haired girl with a spine made of steel.

Maybe nothing would come of this feeling. Maybe it had nothing to do with Alice Elizabeth Leighton. I didn't know and I didn't care. What I did know was, in seconds lasting as long as seasons, I was just grateful as fuck to feel . . . well, anything.

Then I remembered. She thought I was an asshole.

She was right, of course, but I wanted in there anyway.

"I don't care how famous he is," I could hear her sister talking above the music. Alice had her back to me, her lustrous hair cascading down her back, curling at the ends. "I think he's a dirty old coot and it's totally weird what he's asking of you."

"It's not just me. Everyone who signed up had to make the same commitment. Frankly, I was lucky to get a spot."

What the hell is she talking about?

"It's just . . . just . . . so personal!" Her sister gulped down the rest of her wine. "Can't you just make something up? How's he going to know the difference anyway? Wait, he doesn't expect you to *video* yourself having sex, does he?"

Ah, hell no. That was it. "Dixie, you're in New York for, what, five minutes and already you've got some perv trying to take advantage of you?"

Alice turned around and, for a flash of a second, I saw it: her eyes going wide, her pupils dilating, those bow-shaped lips gaping. Her gaze racked over me, as real as any touch.

That is, until she remembered she wasn't supposed to like me. Then she scrunched up that cute-as-hell, pixie nose while giving her most vicious, evil stink-eye.

It was adorable as fuck.

"It's not like that," she said, coming right up to me and pointing her finger into my chest. "And you have no say whatsoever in what I do or don't do."

She may not have liked me, but she sure as hell was attracted to me. *That's fine*, I thought. *I don't need much else.*

But I made the mistake of showing that her reaction pleased me and I felt all of Alice shut down, hiding behind a perturbed expression. She folded her arms across her breasts as she jutted her chin up.

I had to bite the inside of my cheek in order not to laugh because I was sure this was her being a badass. And I had already pissed her off enough. It was time to get on her good side.

That said, I was still me, which meant I had to be, well, a smart-ass.

"See anything you like?"

She let out a sound between a snort and a laugh. "Why is it that everything coming out of your mouth sounds like a come on?"

I took a step closer, my hands deep in my pockets so I wouldn't reach out and touch her, something I really wanted to do. "Don't worry. It's not a habit. I only sound like that when I see something I like."

"Oh dear Lord, first you're yelling at me to get a move-on and now you're all up in my space, letting your flirty beast out."

I stroked the side of my beard, shaking my head. "I promise you, sweet Alice, I've got one hell of a beast for you, but he doesn't flirt. He conquers."

She rocked a half step back. It was like we were doing the waltz in reverse.

"Well, maybe some kingdoms aren't looking to be conquered. Maybe they're looking for someone who appreciates the treasure already possessed within their walls."

"That's the difference between a prince and a king," I said, not doing a good job of hiding the smile I was sporting.

"Oh, I can't wait to hear this," she said, her eyes alit, coy and mischievous. Her lipstick was fresh, but she still rubbed her lips together.

Fuck but I wanted in there.

I got nearer, letting my mouth get close to her ear. I heard her breath hitch and witnessed the pulse point in her neck pick up speed.

"A prince is some spoiled, entitled jerkoff who thinks the world catering to him is his due. A king, on the other hand, understands that while he is the one who rules, he is also responsible for those in his charge. He is beholden to them, for their welfare."

She blinked a couple of times and swallowed, just staring up at me.

"In other words, he only conquers what he can care for. Otherwise, he's no better than a savage."

She pressed a hand to her cheek, then her forehead. "It's kind of hot in here. Don't you think it's too warm?"

I ignored her comment. "So, what do think?" I directed towards my art piece.

"Oh, well, I don't know a lot about art," she said as her eyes searched for her sister, who was no longer standing by her side. Her sister still had

Alice in her line of vision, but she was chatting with a random suit.

I reached out and took her chin between my thumb and forefinger, moving her head back in my direction.

"This isn't an academic symposium where you have to espouse a thesis-worthy response," I told her, reluctant to let go, but doing it anyway. I wanted to draw her in, not scare her off. "Just tell me what it makes you feel."

She was wearing her hair down, which I liked a lot, especially since she was close enough to the art to be right under one of the spotlights. The light made her glow even brighter. She ran both hands through that thick hair, grabbing it in a bunch at the nape of her neck as she turned towards the art on the wall.

This was the second time I'd seen her, and both times she'd worn a curve hugging, retro dress, like something out of a pinup calendar. Her body was made for the style, with those full, gorgeous breasts, tiny waist and heart-shaped ass—the one I'd gotten to study in detail when she was hauling her stuff out of that cab. As she turned, the skirt of her dress swooshed by me, a whisper of a touch I felt through my jeans.

She didn't respond right away and, for the first time in a long while, I was on edge about what someone else thought of my work. Of course, she didn't know it was mine—I didn't sign this one—which meant I would probably get a truthful answer out of her.

Although something told me Alice would give it to me straight regardless.

"It's compelling," she said. "I like how the artist carved part of the figure out of the drywall plaster while using ordinary objects to share what's going in the subject's internal and external realities. I get the sense he feels . . . stuck, unable to change his life or the world around him."

And we have a winner. She nailed exactly what I was going for.

"Who is the artist?"

I shrugged. Maybe someday I'll tell her. "Does it matter?"

That one got me my first sweet smile. "No, I suppose it doesn't."

"C'mon," I placed my hand on the small of her back. "Let's get your stuff."

"Oh right . . . wait! I need to let my sister know where I'm going."

"I'm happy to follow wherever you go," I said.

You have no idea how much.

I caught a hint of a grin, which she tried to hide by ducking her head and letting her hair fall forward. It made me wonder how all that hair would feel in my grip as I fucked her from behind.

We got to where her sister was standing: she was playing with her auburn tendrils and listening to some dipshit. Alice was several inches shorter than her sister and they looked nothing alike. Alice kept trying to interject, but whoever this suit was, he was rambling like a toddler on a sugar high.

So of course, I just started talking over him. "I hear you're the guardian ad litum for the evening. I'm taking your sister upstairs to get her stuff. I'm assuming you two are a package deal and you'd want to come along. Am I right?"

I got a perfectly arched eyebrow in response. "That is correct."

The guy started moving his jaw from side to side, obviously getting all bent out of shape that we were interrupting his limp dick version of game. Alice's sister wasn't my type, but she was gorgeous, so I didn't know why she was even bothering with this idiot.

"She looks like a big girl to me. She doesn't need a babysitter."

Alice interjected. "You have the manners of a feral goat and everyone knows goats are the assholes of the animal kingdom. C'mon Caroline."

Shit, that's funny. I smiled to myself. *Though she be but little, she is fierce.*

"Uh, she's not going anywhere, bitch." I could see the veins popping out of the shitgibbon's temples.

Caroline pulled out of his grip. "Do not. Touch. Me."

"Not a good move, Wall Street," I informed him.

"Who the fuck are you?" he spat back. I started laughing because, I had to hand it to him, he was stupid but spunky. With bare feet, I'm six-four and I bench two-eighty. This guy was five-nine on his tippy toes.

I made a mental note to tell Ingrid we needed to be stricter about the guest list because this whole moment sponsored by Frat Boys R Us was a big bag of bullshit.

"Oh, I get it. You wandered in here by mistake." I gestured towards the front. "Go out that door, make a right and one block down is the Viagra doc, and then a couple blocks more you'll find Hooters, where I'm sure you and the rest of your knuckle-dragging jizztrumpets have gathered for a chest-bumping, degenerative good time. Don't forget to bring the roofies so you'll be sure to score."

"You're a real smart-mouthed motherfucker, aren't you?" He started swinging before I had a chance to answer. I pushed Alice and her sister behind me while maneuvering out of the way.

"That's some pansy ass shit you're throwing there, Wall Street," I tapped my chin with my fingers, jutting it straight out. "Here, I'll make it easy for you. C'mon, try again."

His whole face turned beet red, but I could tell from his stance he wasn't giving up yet. Moron.

"I'm going to enjoy beating the ever-living *shit* out of you!" He reared his fist back and swung at me. I ducked in time for him to hit one of the cement columns.

I knew that sound well. The asshole had just shattered most of the bones in his hand.

"Motherfucker! You broke my hand! I'm suing your ass for everything's you've got."

"Annnnd THAT'S my cue," Ingrid signaled one of the bouncers who grabbed his arm and wrenched it behind his back.

A crowd had formed. I shook my head, making a tsk tsk sound. "'Roid rage is real, ladies and gentleman." Everyone cracked up.

"You can't take me on yourself? You need these goons to do your dirty work?" He was trying to goad me, but I didn't flinch.

"Hey, fuck nugget, I gave you a clear shot and you *still* couldn't hit me. So go ahead, sue me all ya want. I've got a cousin I put through Harvard Law who's like my personal concili re. He's a pitbull who needs a new chew toy."

The idiot paled and they carted him out of there. Drumming fingers on folded arms caught my eye.

"Should I even ask why you were bothering with that asswipe?" Ingrid asked.

"Oh, c'mon! If this had been even a few months ago, I would've pummeled that shitbag and gotten dragged into court. I'm totally growing and maturing over here."

"Alright, *fine*, you're emotional maturation is one standard deviation above impulsive toddler."

"That's better," I said, turning my attention to Alice. "You're okay?"

"Oh, I'm right as rain," she answered, turning to her sister. "Can you please tell me why on God's green earth were you even *talking* to that idiot?"

Caroline stared at Alice for a couple of beats before her gaze went skyward, all while shaking her head.

"I swear, sister, you could throw yourself down on the ground and you'd still miss."

"Is that right?"

Caroline gave her an exasperated look. "I was steering clear so that you and green eyes over there could talk, without me looming over you. I could've been talking to a totem pole for all I cared."

That was enough to make Alice blush. She had this luminescent, porcelain skin, the kind that probably burned easily from the sun—or in this case, embarrassment.

I rested my hand on her back. "Hey," I said low enough for just her to hear me.

Prussian blue eyes met mine, sending an electric current down my spine.

"You haven't got one thing to be embarrassed about. It was cool of your sister to give me a chance to talk to you. Because honestly? That's all I've been wanting to do, since the moment I met you—and that desire only doubled after I went through your bag."

"Really?" she asked, her soft voice making it harder to resist her.

"Christ, not this again," Ingrid muttered.

That caught my attention. "What was that?"

I had my hand on Alice's shoulder, which was exactly where Ingrid's eyes darted to before giving me the stink eye.

"You know *exactly* what I mean," she said.

Alice moved out of my touch. I may have growled.

"Whatever, don't say I didn't warn you." She gave Alice a cold look before she headed off. I scrubbed my hands over my face.

"What was that about?" Caroline asked, her eyes shooting daggers at me.

I let out a harsh exhale. "Nothing to do with either of you."

"Is she your girlfriend or something?" Alice asked, her confusion written all over her face.

"No, she's my friend and my assistant."

"Why don't I believe you?" her sister asked.

"You should. Because I don't lie, sometimes to my own detriment," I said, feeling annoyed at Ingrid for being so overprotective. I knew she was just looking out for me, but having this conversation was annoying the shit out of me.

Neither girl moved. *Shit, I'm blowing this before it's even started.*

I gentled my expression. "Ingrid is like family and her reaction is part of a long story. One I'd rather not get into right now." *Or ever.*

With just a quick glance, they communicated something between them. A spark of envy ignited in the center of my chest. It had always been just my mom and me. Ingrid was like a sister to me, but it wasn't the same as having someone you've grown up with your whole life.

"Let me also say I'm sorry Ingrid threw some 'ugly' your way. She's actually a sweetheart."

Alice's head jerked, but then she beamed at me. I was starting to like earning those smiles already. "I'm going to give you that redirect, but only because you incorporated some of my Southern charm into your Yankee vernacular, City."

"Are you ever going to use my name?"

"Oh I like City better. Suits you."

"If I do this right, you may think Dare's the better fit."

"You know, I still think you're arrogant."

"Noted."

"And rude," she added.

"Got it."

"Just so you know, I'm just getting my stuff and then I'm out of here."

"Your choice, but I'm hoping that's not all you want."

Alice guffawed. "Should I even ask what else you're hoping I'm going to want?"

I felt my cock stir. "Don't ask me that," I said. "But after I get that weightlifting kit you call a purse back to you, I'd like to drop your sister off and then take you out."

I heard her breath hitch as she sunk her teeth into the swell of her bottom lip.

It may have been the sexiest thing I've seen in a long, long while.

Until she opened her mouth.

"I don't think so. I've got an early day tomorrow."

Okay, that was not the answer I was expecting. Either this woman wasn't into me, and I had read the signals wrong or she was into playing games.

Or something else was holding her back from what she really wanted: Me.

My instinct was telling me it was the latter, but I was going to proceed with cautious levity.

"Do you have a boyfriend? Girlfriend?"

"Appreciate you not making assumptions, but no to both," she said.

I shot a glance over to her sister. "Let the record reflect that Ms. Leighton has officially turned me down."

"So noted, my sister's an idiot." Caroline was enjoying the scene even more than I was, which only made Alice back hand her sister's upper arm.

"Ow! That hurt!" she said while rubbing her bicep.

"Serves your right," Alice said.

"Don't let her diminutive size fool ya," she said. "She is freakishly strong. Like a mutant, really."

"I'll keep that in mind, but I think I'm still willing to risk my physical safety." I pointed towards the elevator with my chin. "Let's get your stuff."

She shoved one hand deep inside her side pocket while weaving the other with Caroline's. *Hmm, sister as human shield, that's a new one,* I thought.

We went up to the business office where I kept everything of consequence under lock and key, noticing the two of them having full conversations without saying a word.

"By the way, your sister's strong as an ox because she's hauling a bag around that makes the Sherpas of Mount Everest look like lazy fucks."

"Southern women are always stronger than they look," Caroline said.

"Yeah, I saw Steel Magnolias too, honey. The pretty girl died. It was sad."

Alice gave me the stink eye. "Really, Dare?"

Man, I loved my name in her mouth, rolling off her tongue. I wished she was moaning it instead of barking it, but whatever.

"I swear I'm a good guy under all this curmudgeon gruff," I said, giving her my most sincere smile. "Are you sure you have to turn in early?"

"Um, I'll wait by the elevator," Caroline said while walking out of the room, leaving us alone for the first time. I wanted to invite Alice for a drink up in my apartment, but I knew that'd be pushing it.

She seemed to be studying my expression. Hoisting her bag onto her shoulder, she took a step closer.

"You know the game two truths and a lie?"

This was coming out of left field. "Sure I do."

"So, let's play a round and I'll see if you can fool me."

"What, like right now?"

She gave me this suggestive, lopsided smile.

"Don't think. Just say yes."

Damn, she was driving me wild. "You are, by far, the sexiest woman I've met in a while," I groaned, getting into her space, my large hands resting on the curves of her hips.

She slid her hands up my arms, bracing them on my chest. "Let's hear 'em. I'm ready."

Oh that's right . . . she wanted two truths and a lie. I was good at this little game.

"Okay, number one: I turned down a full scholarship to M.I.T and went to art school instead. My mom didn't speak to me for a week. Number two: I didn't lose my virginity until I was eighteen, but it was with my high school English teacher the day after graduation, so it was totally worth the wait. And number three: It's in my will that when I die, I'm to have a Viking funeral. You know, the whole launching of fiery arrows to my body on a boat out at sea thing."

Her brows went up. "That's quite a list."

"You bet your sweet ass it is," I smiled, but it faded fast because she backed away. "What's wrong?"

"You're really good at this game."

She was complimenting me without it feeling like much of a compliment.

"Annnnd?"

She repositioned the bag strap on her shoulder, looking towards the door before meeting my eyes.

"What? Tell me," I said.

She let out something between a huff and sigh. "You're too good at this game. I couldn't tell which ones were the truth and which one was the lie."

Now I was confused. "Isn't that the whole point of the game?"

"In theory," she said, a flash of uncertainty clouding her eyes. "But if I can't tell when you're lying, this early in knowing you, without any emotional attachment, then how am I ever going to know once I'm involved with you?"

What. The. Fuck. "You're shitting me, right?"

She straightened her spine. "No, I am not 'shitting' you," she said. "Listen, I appreciate you getting my bag back to me. But I'm done with trying to make sense of men and their Mad Hatter nonsense. So, thanks for the drink invite, but I'm good solo."

And then, wouldn't you know it, the little firecracker walked out on me.

Five

> "Alice got so much into the way of expecting nothing
> but out-of-the-way things to happen, that it seemed quite
> dull and stupid for life to go on in the common way."
> ~Lewis Carroll, *Alice in Wonderland*

Alice

"SO, LET ME get this straight. Dare Grangeworth—*the* Dare Grangeworth—is the guy who found your purse in the back of the cab. Am I getting this right so far?"

I let out a harsh breath. "You know that part already, Ray-Ray."

"Wait a second, Dare Grangeworth? The famous artist?" Lulu piped up before sipping her tea in a cup almost as large as her head. We were having Sunday brunch at our favorite place, Gallow Green, on the rooftop of the McKittrick Building.

"Lo sé, está loca!" Rayna said.

"I am not crazy," I snapped.

"I didn't recognize him in person, but I sure know the name Dare Grangeworth." My sister had to contribute. She eyed my plate, noticing I wasn't really eating. "He's a real catch, Alice. Handsome, successful . . ."

Rayna interrupted. "I hear he can be an asshole."

My sister shrugged. "Well, I don't know about that. He was a bit rough around the edges when we first met him, but I thought he was funny and charming, in a New York kind of way—exactly Alice's type."

"I heard on the subway the other day that Dare Grangeworth was asked by NYC magazine to be on the cover of their most eligible bachelor issue, but he turned them down," Lulu said.

I plunked back in my seat, folding my arms in front. "Do y'all have to keep saying his name over and over?"

"I don't know why you couldn't of at least had a drink with the man the other night," Caroline said. "He did keep your pocketbook safe *and* sent a car for us both ways."

"Yeah, I was there, Caroline. And, for the last time, no one but old blue-hairs call it a 'pocketbook.'" I picked up my fork and shoved some of my huevos rancheros into my mouth so I wouldn't say anything I would regret.

"All right, so why didn't you want to go out with him?" my sister asked, stirring sugar into her coffee.

I eyed her. "Geez, I don't know. Maybe because I just got here and the last thing I want to do is get wrapped up a guy, especially one who's kind of famous."

"Oh honey, he's not 'kind of' famous. Dare Grangeworth is not 'kind of' anything. That man is full throttle, whatever he does." Rayna informed me.

I sipped my herbal tea. "All the more reason to stay away. Can we talk about something else?"

Lulu gave a quick, half wave. "I've got some news."

"Great! Let's hear it." I was more than anxious to take the focus off of me.

She threaded her pale blond hair behind her ear. "So Beck has agreed to invest in my latest invention. In fact, I leave for California at the end of the week to meet with his West Coast team."

"That's amazing!" I told her, giving her a hug.

Caroline clapped like an excited seal. "Congratulations! We need some mimosas right quick!"

"Forget the juice, chica. Necesitamos champán!"

A waiter came right over and, before we had a chance to do anything, Rayna had paid for the whole thing with her black Amex card. She told him something else in Spanish that none of us could catch. When he returned with a bottle of Veuve Clicquot Rosé, we caught on fast.

"Rayna, this is too much," Lulu said, although I noticed a smile curling at the corner of her mouth. She was right about Ray-Ray going overboard, but I also knew if our little group didn't give Lulu some love and recognition, no one else in her life would do it.

"Don't make me pull out my crop and make you my bitch," Rayna winked, signing for the bill. The waiter coughed, hitting the center of his chest with his fist, excusing himself before scurrying off.

"Do you think he recognized you?" Lulu asked, her eyes alight; she was living proof of the saying, 'it's always the quiet ones' because she thought Rayna being a professional Dominatrix was the bomb diggity.

"*No lo* sé, *conejito*. Probably not. She shrugged and lifted her glass. "Never mind him. Let's toast!"

We lifted our glasses. "To Lulu, our gadget guru!" she said.

"To Lulu!" We all clicked our glasses just as the most perfect, sweet breeze swirled around us.

EVERYONE ELSE TOOK off after brunch, but I decided to walk home solo, enjoying the last days of Indian summer before I got to experience my first autumn in New York. Then my phone rang, and I knew my mini-vacay was over.

Because whoever was actually making a phone call instead of texting or emailing was definitely over forty and, therefore, a guaranteed scorch on my vibe. I pulled my phone out of my pocket and, sure enough, I knew nothing good could come from a call from my university, especially on a Sunday.

"Hello?" I said.

"Hello. Who is this?"

I snickered. "You're the one calling me, buddy."

"Well, I know that," he sounded annoyed already. "But who. Are. You?"

Then I heard a sound, like someone was sucking on a pipe, followed by a wet, retching, and disgusting cough. Unfortunately, I knew it well.

"Hi, Professor Bails. It's Alice Leighton. Happy Sunday to you."

Happy Sunday? What was I, one of the little people in Munchkin Land? Who talks like that?

"Oh yes, I remember now."

Good for you, dude. You're paid six figures and teach one class a year. Glad you can remember whom you're calling. On a Sunday.

"I'm phoning because I have yet to receive your case study proposal. Many of your classmates are already recording data. Did I make a mistake in allowing a first year into my seminar?"

"No!" I called out, making people walking by turn their heads. I mouthed 'sorry' and continued. "No professor, you did not make a mistake. I had some delays, because of my living situation, but that's handled now."

He let out a loud sigh. "The whole point of the case study, Mizzz Laaay-tonnn," he spoke like I had been dropped on the head one too many times, "is to record how the stressors of life affect your sex life, so you will experience what your future clients go through—*not* to wait until your moon is in Aquarius with everything aligned to your preference."

He wasn't done. Professor Bails rattled on for at least eight more blocks. For someone who was seventy, looked eighty, and sounded over a hundred, he had a lot more lungpower than I would have thought.

I turned the last corner and headed down my block.

"And lastly, Mizzz Laaay-tonnn, I took a chance on you because you came from Chapel Hill with such high praise, and well, I thought you would be up to the challenge this level requires, but if you can't . . ." he kept droning on and on, the same thing over and over. Where was that phlegmy cough when I needed it?

I wasn't wearing my glasses or contacts, but there seemed to be a massive hulk of man on the steps leading up to my building.

Dark hair and a beard.

Sunglasses.

It was Dare.

The Dare Grangeworth, as all my girls liked to remind me.

And he was sitting on my front stoop.

I didn't know if my moon was in Aquarius or square dancing into Saturn, but something was finally aligning, doing a hop-skip right to my doorstep. And as soon as I got close enough to see, as soon as his gaze met mine, he smiled as if the one thing he had lost had finally been found.

I stopped just short of where Dare was seated, with his long legs stretched in front of him. Without taking my eyes off of him, I said, "Professor Bails? Yes, I hear you. I'll have my proposal on your desk by tomorrow morning."

Dear sweet Jesus, was I really going to do this?

Six

"My dear, here we must run as fast as we can, just to stay in place.
And if you wish to go anywhere you must run twice as fast as that."
~Lewis Carroll, *Alice in Wonderland*

Dare

NEW YORK IS filled with goodbye girls. I should know. I was raised by
one.

Being reared by a single mother was like getting a front row seat to a
never-ending movie called 'Really Stupid Shit Men Do.' It probably didn't
help that I humored my mom by spending too many nights home with
her, watching a shit-ton of rom-coms. Sure, some were mind-numbing
drivel, but seeing her light up with every happy ending made it worth it.
They also offered a younger, pain-in-the-ass version of myself an ersatz
education in how to win the girl of your dreams.

I wasn't sure if Alice was that girl, but she intrigued the hell out of
me. And I knew we had chemistry. She had turned me down because of
that two truths and a lie 'test.' Now, a lot of guys would've heard that
nonsense and written her off as 'crazy' or 'high-maintenance,' but those

dipshits didn't know dick about women.

Maybe I didn't either, but I knew this: Most women weren't 'crazy.' Trust me, I'd been with one who was, and there's a big fucking difference. I'd doled out enough tissues, my arm around my mom as she cried at the end of every sappy movie to learn that while grand gestures were cool, just showing up and proving you don't scare so easy was worth even more.

That said, if Neil Simon's *Goodbye Girl* is playing on cable, I'm going to stop what I'm doing and watch until the end. Because when Richard Dreyfus exchanges his first-class seat to stardom for two economies, so Marsha Mason can finally get out of the rain and be with a man who knew that she—and her daughter, Lucy—were worth a hell of a lot more . . . well, it gets to this die-hard New Yorker every time.

That's what I was thinking about as I spotted Alice turn the corner, phone to her ear, walking home. The air hurt going in because, yeah, she was that beautiful. I was waiting for her, sitting on the steps of her building, hoping like hell she'd find my impromptu visit a sign of my tenacity and romantic worth, instead of as a prompt to download a restraining order on her phone ASAP.

I was here to prove I was not so easily dissuaded. But before you give me a starring role in your next Hallmark Movie of the Week, I should admit to something: I've been cheating. Again.

This time, I didn't have one of her notebooks, but I did have her sister's cell. I texted her this morning, asking where Alice would be later today and if she thought I was wasting my time.

Her words: *My sister is as stubborn as a mule, but she likes you. She just won't admit it yet. Don't make me regret breaking sister code. You hurt her, I break you.*

At least I had Caroline in my corner. Sort of. According to her, I was going to need all the help I could get.

Meanwhile, I finally had Alice in my sights: walking with a natural sway in her hips, glasses perched on top of her head. Despite her eyes focused in my general direction, I could tell she hadn't spotted me yet.

She wasn't in one of her usual cinched-in pin-up girl dresses, and while I got off on those, I was just as captivated by her in a pair of faded jeans and boots. She was also wearing a peasant blouse in a shade of caramel that matched the highlights in her russet brown hair. The clothes were earthy and relaxed but she layered her look with a lot of thin necklaces, stacked rings and bangle bracelets in all shades of metal, giving her an urban edge.

I was paying close attention to all the details because there was a strong possibility that she'd take one look at me, throw a fit, and toss me out. Lord knew if the laws of karma applied, I'd deserve it. So, I was taking note in case this day ended up as just a memory.

As she got closer, I heard the tail end of her call. Her eyes locked with mine.

"Professor Bails? Yes, I know you've been patient . . ."

She shook her head and rolled her eyes while saying it. I stifled a laugh, making her face crack open with a big grin.

"Right, well, I have someone in mind. What I mean is, I met someone . . . yes, I've arranged to talk to him . . . yes, *today.*"

She pointed to the phone and mouthed *what an asshat.*

"I'll have my proposal on your desk by tomorrow morning. Right, no delays . . . I understand . . . yes, sir. Goodbye."

She ended the call and stared at the phone in her hand for a second before a mask of determination set in.

"Whatever you've got in that gorgeous head of yours, forget it," I told her as I leaned forward, forearms resting on my knees with the arm of my sunglasses hanging from my teeth. "Because, despite what you may have read about me online, I'm not, in fact, into 'the group thing,' drugs of any kind, or hooking up with random people from Craigslist."

Alice let out a snort-laugh. "I haven't Googled you, but I'm thinking I've been missing out."

"Trust me, you haven't. You can believe about half of what you read about the New York art world in the press and even less when it comes to me. Most of it is smoke and mirrors, and I'll be the first one to admit I've used it to my advantage."

The sun got lost behind a cloud cluster. I tucked my sunglasses inside my jacket pocket.

"Well, so . . . you're not into any of that?"

I cocked a brow.

"You're not," she said under her breath, kicking the bottom of the bannister with the toe of her boot. "What are you doing here, anyway?"

You know why I'm here. I stood up and came down a couple of steps so I wouldn't tower over her more than I already did. "I wanted to know if you'd like to take a walk with me."

She looked confused. "You want to take a walk?"

"Honestly, I could take it or leave it. What I really want is to spend time with *you*. But since you already turned down drinks, I thought suggesting anything more might scare you off."

She was staring up at me, those blue eyes the color of a Caribbean I'd kill to drown in, as long as I was with her. My chest expanded, an ocean of air swirling through me.

Slow down, man. You still know nothing about her and she's probably wary for reasons of her own.

"What I don't want is to make you uncomfortable in any way," I went on. "Tell me you're not interested, and I'm gone. That's a promise."

Alice shoved her hands in her jean pockets while looking down at her boots. "It was a lousy thing to do . . . that whole two truths and a lie test I put you through the other day."

I didn't answer. I could tell she needed to get whatever was bugging her off her chest more than I needed to hear an apology.

Alice raised her head and met my eye. "I played a zero-sum game and you still texted my sister in an attempt to track me down and ask me out."

She let out something between a sigh and a groan. "I'm sorry about the other night, Dare. It's not cool to make you pay for someone else's bullshit."

I shrugged. "We've all got baggage, Alice," I said.

"I also need to ask you a favor."

"Shoot," I said.

She blew out a breath, tucking her folded arms closer to her while staring off. "Let's go upstairs. I need the illusion of privacy in order to ask you what I need to ask you."

This must be a doozy. I stepped to the side. "Lead the way," I said.

She nodded, taking out a key card. She waved it in front of the censor and the door clicked open.

I followed her inside, the whole time we were waiting, riding the elevator and walking into her apartment, I was trying to figure out what she was working up the nerve to ask me. I knew she was studying to be some kind of sex expert, so that helped narrow down what the favor could be. By the time we got inside, I had quite a list:

1.   Donating my dick to science, hopefully after I'm dead.

2.   Wanting me to try out some new form of dude birth control, one known to shrink my balls down to tiny kumquats.

3.   A new pill to help frat boys combat whiskey dick.

"Would you like something to drink?" she asked as she shrugged off her jacket.

"No, I'm good," I told her, standing just inside the door.

She smiled and shook her head. "You can come in. Have a seat and stay awhile," she said, motioning to the navy loveseat. "I'm getting myself some tea. You sure you don't want something?"

She was flitting around her kitchen, not looking my way. I was guessing she needed to make it more than I needed to drink it.

"Sure, whatever you're having," I said, tossing my jacket onto the plaid side chair. I looked around, noticing the place was a hodge podge of styles, but all about comfort. The sitting area and kitchen was one big room, a partial island with barstools demarcating the space. Off to the side was a nook, where they could've fit a small dining set, but instead it held a twin bed, a skinny dresser and a hanging rack with a few pieces of clothing.

"Is that your room?" I asked, giving a head nod towards the bed nook.

She barely glanced over. "Uh, yeah. It's fine. I'm hardly ever at home."

Typical New York half 'bedroom.' I didn't miss those days.

She filled a teakettle and turned on the stove burner.

"Putting it in the microwave is faster, you know," I told her.

The corner of her mouth quirked. "Faster isn't always better. Besides, my nana was convinced microwaves made the water taste funny."

"That's such a grandma thing to say. Mine never allowed cursing or malicious gossip in her kitchen because she thought it put bad mojo in her sauce."

Her shoulders shook with silent laughter as she got cream out of the fridge and poured it into one of those ridiculous white ceramic cow dispensers.

And she's still not asking me what she wanted to ask. How bad is this favor anyway?

"So, I'm guessing you came to New York for that fancy sex program."

The kettle went off. She turned to grab an extra mug out of a high cupboard, her blouse raising enough so I caught view of the full curve of her ass and a sliver of creamy skin. I bit my top lip so I wouldn't groan.

She took the kettle off the burner, then placed the mug next to her bone china cup and saucer; something dainty next to something clunky. *Like the two of us: that's fitting.*

"It's a clinical psych degree, specializing in human sexuality studies."

"Right . . . like I said . . . sex."

She eyed me while placing the tea bags in and slowly pouring the hot water over them. "I'm thinking a man who earned a full ride to M.I.T. doesn't really think I'm in a 'sex' program."

I chuckled, not surprised she'd known that was one of my truths. "What can I say; I like fucking with you."

I'd also really like to fuck you, but we'll get to that soon enough.

She placed the mug of tea in front of me, along with Elsie the cow and a matching ceramic bear filled with honey.

This woman killed me; Alice didn't even have a real bedroom, but she had designated receptacles for her tea crap.

She drained the bag and set it aside before letting out an audible sigh. "Okay . . . wow, this is harder to ask then I expected."

"I came up with a whole list on the way up here. Bet whatever you're going to ask me is far better than some of the shit I made up."

"What did you . . . ?" She shook her head and waved me off. "No, I don't want to know." She put both palms flat on the counter, staring down at her teacup. She closed her eyes for a couple of seconds, then finally opened them.

The fiery determination had returned. *There she is*, I thought.

"Okay, I told you about what I'm studying and, since it's a doctoral program, well, it means I've got years ahead of me. I am determined not to take a decade to finish my degree."

"I can understand that. Go on," I encouraged.

She gave a hint of a nod. "Right, so there's this year-long seminar. Well, it's not a seminar, per se. It's more like a qualitative study with me as the guinea pig."

That raised both brows. "Come again?"

"Professor Aaron Bails is a leader in the field of human sexuality. He was one of the last students of Alfred Kinsey and still conducts research through the Kinsey Institute. Anyway, he believes there's no way we can ever truly help people with their sexual dysfunctions or embrace their proclivities unless we've gone through the process ourselves . . ."

I was waiting for her to drop the bomb.

" . . . which means in order to be part of this seminar, I need to be having regular sex with a partner for a minimum of four months . . . and I need to document what occurs, not in a salacious way . . . no video or anything like that. But both my partner and I need to be brutally honest about what we experience and what we fantasize about . . . and I want it to be you."

And there it was . . . BOOM.

I was the guy who usually had a sarcastic retort, but this time?

I had nothing.

"We don't have to be monogamous, as long as we're practicing safe sex. And it's not like we'd be 'dating' or anything. I'm not going to 'catch feelings' if that's what you're worrying about."

I barked out a laugh as I rubbed my hand over my face. "I've got to admit, that was not what I expected you to ask me."

She worried the corner of her bottom lip with her teeth. "I understand if you want time to think about it."

I didn't need time. I needed answers.

"Okay, let me get this straight," I said, rubbing the furrow along my forehead. "This ass clown wants to hear the details of your sex life?"

She grimaced. "Not in the way you're thinking. Professor Bails wants all his students to explore their own sexuality. It's the chance to dig deep into what makes us tick, to go down the rabbit hole, so to speak. How can we expect to help others if we don't go through the work ourselves?"

I looked down at the mug of tea she had made for me, wishing it were a cup of strong coffee. Bourbon would be even better.

"Makes sense," I said, tugging at the string on the tea bag. "Listen, you know I'm interested in you. I wouldn't have shown up here if I wasn't. But now the whole thing feels, I don't know . . ."

She interrupted. "Forced?"

"Something like that."

Her mouth formed into a perfect 'O' as she lifted her cup and blew on it. I lost some of my brain function as some blood flew south, straight to my dick.

What the fuck is your problem? She's basically saying you can fuck her five ways 'til Sunday and you're ticked off because she didn't take you to dinner and tell you you're pretty first?

But, of course, I'm, well . . . *me*, which meant I needed to pick at the scab some more.

"I know you want to graduate as fast as possible, but wouldn't you prefer to wait until you had, I don't know, someone steady in your life? You know, half the fun is letting something unfold between two people."

She cocked her head. "Who says I'm not letting something unfold? I'm just giving you a heads up there's something extra in it for me."

I stilled as she gave an impish grin, with a glint in her eye.

Bam—a direct hit.

I got off the stool and walked around the kitchen island, liking how her eyes rounded watching me.

"Only one thing left to figure out then," I said.

I didn't hesitate; I drove my fingers deep into her lustrous hair, yanked her towards me and took that pink mouth of hers.

I wasn't gentle, either. I was too hungry, but when her moan vibrated down my throat, I took that as a sign she was good with a little rough. It was barely autumn, but she already tasted like Christmas, nutmeg and spicy cinnamon tea. Sweet with an edge.

Small, delicate hands gripped my shirt at the sides as I felt her soft curves pressed against me. I slid one hand around the back of her neck while letting the other move its way down and around her waist. I pulled her even closer, so tempted to fall on my knees and strip her out of those faded jeans, feast between those thick thighs of hers.

I could do that for days and never feel sated.

I've had people call 'bullshit,' but I swear, I preferred going down on a woman even more than a blowjob. Getting head was great, but I got off on being surrounded by a woman's velvet heat, having her musky scent permeate my senses.

But I wasn't some idiot fuckboy. Never was, never will be. Alice might act as if she was all good with just slamming between the sheets, but I don't know . . . I didn't buy it. Not with her. And I've learned to always trust my gut.

So even though my cock was begging for release, I broke the kiss and tried to catch my breath. It was the same for her. Alice's cheeks were flushed, the pink of her cheeks making the blue of her eyes darken, like a beautiful, Southern storm.

She placed her hand on the center of my chest and smiled as my heart raced beneath her palm.

"You feel what you're already doing to me?" I asked, my voice sounding like gravel, even though everything else felt like liquid silk. "Who knew science could be this much fun?"

Alice nodded through her dazed stare. "Yeah, I think it's safe to say we have chemistry."

We locked eyes and laughed.

And then, her sister walked in-and that killed the mood, as Alice would say, 'right quick.'

Seven

In another moment down went Alice after it, never once
considering how in the world she was to get out again.
~Lewis Carroll, *Alice's Adventures in Wonderland*

Alice

I HAD BEEN so excited that Dare agreed to be part of my case study,
I couldn't get to sleep later that night. So, I did something I swore I'd
never do.

I took one of my sister's Ambien.

I don't know why I thought I would get off easy. Lulu gets Ambien-
esia. Rayna

starts Ambi-texting old boyfriends and if my sister doesn't take hers
at the exact right time, she's a Zambie (zombie because of Ambien hang-
over the next day). I usually refuse to take the stuff because I'm convinced
those lil' fuckers ruin short-term memory.

And dear Lord, that voodoo pill knocked me out faster than Floyd
Mayweather did to that poor little MMA fighter man. I mean, I was *out*.
Or at least I thought I was.

"Well, isn't that craptastic," I muttered under my breath.

It was the next morning and I was having a slow start. But that was the least of everything.

"What's wrong?" my sister asked. She was already dressed and ready for the day.

Meanwhile, I looked like something rolled over me in my sleep. I shuffled out of bed towards the bathroom. "It's nothing," I lied. There was no way I was telling her I did the modern-day equivalent of drinking and dialing.

While doing my business, I sat on my 'throne' and read a text exchange I had absolutely no memory of having. Yep. I'm all class and a bucket of chicken.

DARE: *So I know I've agreed to donate my body in the name of science, but are you up for grabbing some dinner before we knock boots?*

ALICE: *I don't mean to sound crass, but just so you know, in case I hadn't made that clear the other day . . . in the name of science . . . I'm a sure thing*

DARE: *Cute. I'm still taking you to dinner*

ALICE: *Wait a sec. I am not looking to date or have a boyfriend. What makes you think I'm going to have dinner with you?*

DARE: *Because my dick's your golden ticket to your doctorate.*

ALICE: *Nice mouth*

DARE: *Wouldn't you like to know*

ALICE: *Actually, I would, which brings me back to getting together later*

DARE: *Yeah, we'll do that. We're also getting dinner*

ALICE: *But why? It's not like I need you to wine and dine me. I can't go through another Chad. I'm not shrinking myself down ever again.*

DARE: *I got that, Dixie and we'll get into that Chad scenario later. I'm assuming he's your ex. But for the now, just because I've agreed to be your lab rat, that doesn't make us animals. Meet you at Blade, @ eight*

ALICE: *Fine, but only because I'm hungry. Do I have popcorn?*

DARE: *I didn't get to memorize the contents of your kitchen, sweet cheeks. So can't help you there.*

ALICE: *That's okay. I'll make biscuits or something.*

DARE: *You're going to make homemade biscuits?*

ALICE: *Yep. Butter and biscuits. Buttering biscuits. Come over and butter my biscuit big boy. Damn, I love an alliteration!*

DARE: *I'm guessing it's past your bedtime. Get some sleep, beautiful.*

ALICE: *You don't want to butter my biscuits?*

DARE: *Did you drink tonight?*

ALICE: *That's a negatory.*

DARE: *Take any pills?*

ALICE: *I'm sleeping with the Earl of Ambien, if that's what you're getting at.*

DARE: *Yeah, that's what I thought. Put the phone down, princess, and I'll check on you later. We'll be having a talk about the Ambien.*

ALICE: *But first, you're going to feed me, right?*

DARE: *Yes ma'am.*

ALICE: *Alright, since you were so stinkin' polite. Good night, Dare to be Square.*

DARE: *Goodnight Alice in Wonderland.*

The minute I walked out of the bathroom, my sister was on me.

"Okay, spill it," she said.

I glanced up from my phone. "Huh?"

She pursed her lips. "You know I hate it when you play dumb."

"I promise, I'm not playing dumb. I'm just more wiped than a whiteboard."

Caroline was dressed in what I called her work uniform: high-waisted, charcoal skirt with a silk cream blouse, low heels with a red, cashmere cardigan and a string of pearls and pearl button earrings. The pearls weren't real, but they were her 'good fakes' so she took good care of them. Her gorgeous mane of auburn hair was pulled back into a bun.

She looked like a schoolmarm, but that was the point. Rayna was always saying Caroline was a natural Domme, even offering to train her, something hordes of women and men would kill for.

I kept talking. "By the way, remind me to never take those pills again," I said. "Earl Ambien made me agree to have dinner with Dare tonight."

Her lips quirked in wry smile. "You're going, right?"

"Yes, sister," I said. "You can relax. He's insisting on a proper date and all."

"Well, I should hope so," she said, her eyes getting soft. "You're my shiny jewel baby. Remember that."

My throat tightened. "Don't start now," I said.

My sister practically raised me and she always called me her 'jewel baby' whenever her maternal side was poking through.

"You know, you didn't have to chase him off yesterday," Caroline went on. "I know I, for one, would've liked to get to know him better."

I gave her a look. "Don't get attached. Dare and I are not going to be a thing."

That earned another displeased look. "You know, not every guy is going to be like Chad, insisting on all your spare time, enlisting his family to groom you into some perfect lil' Stepford bride."

"How would I know that? Chad was my first real boyfriend and I let him monopolize everything," I said, getting angry at myself all over again. "No, I'm here for school, not for anything else. I don't need the distractions."

"We'll see," she said. "Alright, I've got to go and teach a bunch of entitled, Upper East Siders' children how to at least fake being polite."

"I feel your struggle."

There was a knock. "I'll get it," she said.

Caroline grabbed her briefcase and umbrella, looking like a modern Mary Poppins, and opened the door. Rayna was there, in mid knock.

"Hey girl," Caroline said.

"On your way out?" she asked.

"Yeah, but Alice is here."

I waved from the couch. "Hey Ray-Ray," I called out. I loved when she came over.

"Then you're the lucky bitch of the hour," Rayna said as she winked at my sister leaving.

"Bye you two. Have fun," Caroline said as she closed our door.

"Bye!" Rayna and I said in unison.

She sashayed across the room and wiggled herself into our navy loveseat. Judging from her outfit, she was on her way to the gym.

"How is it possible you don't have a stitch of make-up on, hair up in a pony, wearing sweats and you're still the most gorg woman I've ever seen?" I asked while I picked the sleep out of my eyes.

"*Dios mio*," she muttered under her breath. "This is why I no longer have roommates."

I snorted. "Please, you don't have roommates because you don't *need* roommates. Don't you own this building?"

"*Pequeno*, I own this building and two more, one in Spanish Harlem and another in Long Island City. Real estate is my future. I'm not going to want to punish bad little boys my whole life."

"Man, I am in the *wrong* business," I mumbled.

"I know that's right," she said, putting her feet up on the coffee table.

Even with no makeup on, I swear she still looked like a movie star.

Almond shaped, amber colored eyes with natural, long lashes, a mane of expresso-brown, shampoo commercial-worthy hair . . . let's just say, I may measure as straight on the Kinsey Heterosexual-Homosexual Scale, but I still had to tell myself–often—to stop staring.

I'm sure she felt it, but if she did, Rayna knew how to handle people.

"So, how's school going?" she asked.

"It's good," I said as I gestured towards the kitchen. "I'm making myself some tea. Want some?"

"Sure. You know how I like it."

I nodded, getting up, talking over my shoulder. "Everything happens faster here in New York."

Rayna laughed. "No shit, honey. What did you expect?"

I filled the teakettle with our bottled water. Rayna didn't ever drink from the tap. "Yes, I get that, but I feel like I have to wind myself up, like one of those old toys, and everyone's going a million miles a minute while I'm still searching for the 'on' switch."

"So, how are you holding up?"

I shrugged. "I'm fine. I mean, I think I'm running on adrenaline. Most nights I can't wait to come home and crash, but then I think about everything I learned in my seminars that day and the people I've met and then I'm up half the night. Got so bad, I took one of my sister's Ambiens."

She grabbed a throw pillow from behind her back and pitched it in my direction. "Are you crazy? You know that shit's the worst!"

I waved her off. "I know, I know."

"Ugh, the last time I took one of those, I actually texted Brian . . . took me a month to shake him off," she said with a visible shiver. "Soooo needy."

"Yeah, that's not something one wouldn't expect from the AntiChrist of Rock," I said, grabbing the cups and cream. Brian was the real name of Marilyn Manson, whom she dated for a few months last year. She dumped him after he asked her to play 'mean mommy' one too many times.

"Girl, Ambi-texting is a real and surreal problem," she said, getting up and walking over to the kitchen. She leaned a hip against the counter. "Don't you have class today?"

"No, only on Tuesdays and Thursdays, but I'm TA'ing for Professor Whitmore, which means I have a ton of tests to grade today."

"Oh, that's a shame. I came over because I've got this charity event tonight," she said, watching me make her tea. I handed it to her. "Thanks. Want to come?"

We all loved going with Ray-Ray to any of her events or soirees—because they were always the furthest things from typical, even for New York.

"I think I have a date tonight."

She cocked her head to the side. "You think?"

I chuckled. "No, it's definitely a date. I'm supposed to meet Dare at a place called Blade. Have you heard of it?"

She muttered something in Spanish under her breath that I didn't catch. "Honey, he means business if you're going there."

Now I was nervous. "What? Why?"

She shrugged while blowing on her tea. "It's very romantic. And no one will bother him there."

"What do you mean 'bother' him?" I asked.

She sipped her tea and smiled. "You are the only one who makes my tea exactly how I like it."

I smiled.

"It's a shame we're friends. I should've hired you to be my assistant before we did all the bonding," she went on.

"Yeah, I weep for what might have been," I said. "Explain what you meant."

She rolled her eyes. "What I meant was, he's a local celebrity, a big deal in the New York art world," she said, hopping onto one of the kitchen island stools. "I imagine every struggling artist wants his help and most every woman wants a taste of him and his lifestyle."

"Well, not me," I said. "I just need him for my research."

She laughed. "Yes, I heard about that. Your Southern charm game must be strong in order for him to agree to that."

"Please, he's getting to have no-strings sex. I didn't have to sell it that hard."

She gave me a look over the rim of her teacup. "He's not the typical guy, Alice."

"What have you heard? Please don't tell me he's one of your clients," I said while absentmindedly picking at my cuticles. She reached across the island and play-slapped my hands.

"Stop that," she ordered. "You have beautiful hands. Don't ruin them by picking them to death."

It was like I had another big sister. "Fine."

Her gaze bore into mine, in a way that told me she was exceptionally good at what she did for a living. I held her eye, even though I was almost really to kneel and say 'yes, mistress' just to make her stop staring.

"First of all, no, Dare Grangeworth is not a client, so relax. That doesn't mean I don't know something about him. But you need to decide, going in, how much you want to know. And I ask because I hesitate to take away Dare's opportunity to tell his stories for himself. That's an important part of getting to know someone."

"That's a good point," I said, leaning my forearms on the counter. "And usually, I'm right as rain on letting things unfold in an organic way. But I'm also a curious, curious girl and I'd like to know a lil' something-something going into tonight."

"I get that," Rayna said, a patient smile on her pretty face. "I'll give you this: from what I've heard, he doesn't sleep around and he's not casual about sex, despite what you would find if you Googled him."

"Noted," I said. "What would I find if I Googled him?"

She shrugged. "Early in his career, the press depicted him as the Grangeworth prodigal son who had grown from boy genius to art-rock-god, with a voracious, sexual appetite."

I felt the blood drain from my head.

She eyed me. "Hey, most of that isn't true, Alice. He was working the press, building a brand the art world would want–and it worked. Listen, he's an amazing artist, but that's not enough here. You could line the trashcans of New York with all the talent that's here. Dare knew that and made it work for him."

Her phone beeped and she held up a finger. "Hold on a sec." She read the text, her eyes went wide, but she smoothed her expression.

"What's up? Is everything okay?" I asked.

"It will be," she said, in a way that told me not to pry. I had learned early on there was no use trying to cajole or push her into anything. Rayna was a vault no one knew the combination to.

She typed something quickly, then shoved her phone into her pocket. "I've gotta go," she said as she walked towards the door. But she turned back at the last minute. "One more thing sweetie."

"Yeah?"

"You're going to hear about her. Because there's no hearing about Dare without hearing about Chloe. And there's a lot to hear about Dare and Chloe. Just remember this: it wasn't his fault, even though there are some people who would like someone to blame."

And then she left, locking my door behind her.

I sat there, flummoxed.

"What the heck am I supposed to do with that?"

I OPTED FOR something girly and twirly, a dress in a shade of blue I knew would match my eyes. I may have started this thing between us with the singular task of just having sex in the name of science, but his insisting we have a proper date charmed the Southerner in me. His chivalry brought out all my feminine instincts.

I wore my hair down.

I dabbed my one bottle of expensive perfume onto my wrists, along the column of my neck and behind my knees.

I wore the good underwear, the ones without holes, and a coordinated push-up bra.

A girl could lie to herself quite a bit when it came to a man, but if she's wearing matching bra and panties and bothering to shave, well, the jig is up. She's into the guy.

I have to admit, it didn't hurt at all—him insisting on sending a car to pick me up. My name may have been Alice, but Dare Grangeworth made me feel like a Cinderella on the night of the ball.

I rode that high until I walked into the restaurant. One look around at the beautiful people of Manhattan and the surrounding understated elegance—the kind that can only come from having money—and suddenly, I felt like a dressed-up rube.

If you've ever had that dream of showing up to class naked, well, that's pretty much the same feeling I was experiencing. I fidgeted with the thin, rose gold necklace around my neck and smoothed down my dress, mostly to dry my palm sweat.

Always attractive in a date.

The woman at the hostess stand looked twelve. A six-foot-tall tween wearing stilettos. Of course, she was dressed in the requisite New Yorker-black outfit, something I had yet to succumb to. At least she offered a genuine smile when I approached.

"Uh, hi. I'm meeting Dare Grangeworth?"

"Absolutely. Welcome to Blade. Right this way," she said. I followed her into the restaurant. They had a million lit candles and twinkle lights draped everywhere, making the room feel like a winter wonderland—for rich people.

Towards the back, I spotted Dare at a table for two.

Holy hell, he was handsome. If a fairy godmother had swept in and said I could wish for my perfect man, Dare would be the type, a combination of hard and soft, approachable and elusive.

I am in totally over my head.

The minute he took note I was walking his way, he stood up, his gaze raking over me, and I swore I could feel the heat of it all over. And I have to admit, I noticed he didn't even glance twice at the hostess-tween model-skyscraper.

I liked that. Even my ex, Chad, who used to swear up and down I was the only one for him would still furtively check out other women when we went out.

I hated it.

She moved to pull out my chair, but Dare beat her to it.

"I got it," he said.

"Of course, Mr. Grangeworth. Enjoy your evening," she said, leaving.

We both stood there for a minute, gazing at one other. Already, the evening felt different, in a way that both thrilled and terrified me. I kept telling myself I wasn't looking for a relationship, not beyond sex, at least. But whatever was developing between Dare and I already felt like a living entity, with its own heartbeat, one I could feel outside my chest.

"Hi," I said.

"Hey." His smile so wide, his eyes crinkled in the corners, the sweetness of him making something in the center of my chest open in a warm bloom of happy. He gestured towards the chair. "Sit, relax."

I complied, letting him help tuck in my chair as I fanned my skirt out. When he was done, he leaned close and gave a feather light kiss on my cheek. I caught a hint of his scent: sandalwood and fresh-pressed linen. Delicious. I shivered at the touch and, even though I couldn't see it, I felt him smile.

"You look beautiful, Alice," he said. "That color suits you."

"Thanks, City," I said, my crooked grin growing. "As my mama would say, you clean up real good yourself."

He smiled, taking my compliment in stride. Damn, he really was the epitome of virile masculinity, with his lush beard and big hands. I didn't know his art medium, but whatever it was, it made his hands look rough and used.

Hopefully, just like he was in bed.

He was wearing a black suede jacket, cut to fit his muscled, broad shoulders, so wide I wondered if he had to pivot his body when walking through a standard door.

"Can I just say how much I'm loving the aesthetic in here?" I said, trying to get my brain to focus on something—anything—besides him. "Everyone can't help but look good in this light."

He chuckled. "Hate to break it to you, Alice, but you don't need to worry about the lighting concept in any room you enter. You're stunning, the kind of beautiful that makes the rest of us feel ugly."

I rolled my eyes. "I wouldn't go that far, but thanks."

He frowned.

"What?" I asked.

"I was hoping you weren't the kind of woman who couldn't take a compliment."

I gave a slight head tilt. "You're speaking in double negatives."

"And you're redirecting," he said.

I let out a soft laugh. "Apparently, not in a subtle or effective way. But thank you for the compliment."

His smile returned.

The server came over, read the specials including their handcrafted cocktails.

"That all sounds great, but all I really want is a beer," I said. "Whatever you have on tap is fine."

The waiter started reading from a list as long as my arm.

I interrupted. "Just keep it simple. I'll have a Bud Light."

"I'll have the same. And we'll have wine with dinner. I had a bottle of Sequoia Grove Cambium brought over earlier," he said.

"Very good, Mr. Grangeworth. I'll check with the sommelier," the server said, then walked away.

He leaned forward, forearms on the table, the candlelight casting him in a golden glow. I took the folded napkin and fanned it onto my lap, mostly so I had something to do with my hands. Caroline had taught me well, even if our mama never did.

"It's a relief, going out with someone who orders just what she wants, instead of worrying about putting on airs."

I shrugged. "It shows my Southern roots," I said. "My working-class, Southern roots."

"Nothing wrong with that. I'm the same, despite my name."

"What do you mean?" I asked.

Both his brows shot up. "Really?"

I was blank. "Am I missing something?"

He stared, as if he was trying to assess if I was telling tales or shooting straight.

"Dare," I went on. "What is it?"

"I'm just surprised. Not to sound like an ass, but I'm used to people knowing all about me—or at least *thinking* they know all about me before ever having met me."

"Well, I know some," I said, taking a sip of my water.

A wry smile curled his mouth. "Like what?"

"Well, I didn't Google you, but one of my friends did advise me not to believe your manwhore press image. She said there's more to know, but wanted to leave it to you to do the telling," I said.

His expression registered surprise and, judging from how his shoulders dropped, some relief. "Got to say, I like your friend already."

I leaned forward. "Why Mr. Grangeworth. Do you have something to hide? Some deep and dark secret that would make even us Southern gothic characters gasp in horror?"

Something clouded his eyes, something I couldn't read.

But then the server returned. "Here you are," he said, giving us our beers. "I spoke with Henry, our sommelier. He'll be by to serve your wine with dinner."

He handed us menus.

Dare leaned over the table. "Am I safe in assuming my Southern girl enjoys a good steak?"

My heart fluttered, hearing him call me his Southern girl.

"That's affirmative," I said, trying to exude some New York girl cool.

Stop it, Alice. You just got out of a five-year, claustrophobic relationship.

The last thing you need right now is to get caught up in City's larger than life, man-god tractor beam.

And yet, my Judas of a body was reacting against what my brain was instructing. Welcome to me.

"Good," Dare said, handing back his menu. I did the same. "We'll have two of your Wagyu long-bone ribeye, medium rare, with the usual sides." He turned his attention back to me. "It'll be more than an army can eat, but you can take the rest home with you, if you like. I assumed medium-rare is okay?"

"It's perfect," I said.

The waiter asked, "Do you have any allergies, miss?"

I smiled. "Nope. I can eat anything."

"Very good, miss," the server said.

Finally, we were back to just the two of us again.

"Okay, you've got me curious now," I said, taking a healthy sip of my beer. "What did you mean when you said you're working-class, despite your name?"

He scratched the side of his face. "Well, in New York, the Grangeworths are well known. The man who was technically my father owned a healthy chunk of New York real estate, something he inherited from his father."

"Ah, okay," I said.

"My mom—her name is Regina, but everyone calls her Gina—was Douglas Grangeworth's secretary and mistress. They were together for years. That is, until she became pregnant with me. When she wouldn't have an abortion, he broke it off."

His gaze found mine and this time, I saw something there I did recognize: anger, shame, uncertainty.

"We have almost the same story," I said, placing my hand on top of his. "Except substitute rich, real estate magnate father with probably a no-good, bar fly redneck who couldn't hold a job, and then you'd have whoever my dad was. Same story for my sister, Caroline, by the way."

"Yeah?" he said, giving my hand a squeeze, then placing his other hand on top of mine. I felt the warmth of him everywhere.

"Don't get me wrong. My mama's a good woman," I said, "But she's always been a magnet for deadbeats. She wouldn't know how to make a good decision even if you gave her a step-by-step recipe."

He chuckled. "You're funny," he said, smiling.

I shrugged. "Humor's my favorite coping mechanism."

He took that in. "She must miss you a lot, with both of you being here in the city."

I let go of him to take another sip of my beer. "Caroline and I both went to Chapel Hill for college, which is a good few hours away from Devil's Peak, so she's been used to us gone for a while now."

He nodded, turning the glass in his hand. "I went away for school too, but

I came back here as soon as I could. I can't imagine living anywhere else."

"Where did you go to school?" I asked.

"RISD for art school, the Rhode Island School of Design. Before that, Bronx Science. I did well, but my heart was never into math or the sciences. I always knew I wanted to be an artist."

"Takes a lot of guts, to go for something like that."

"Yes and no," he said.

He didn't elaborate.

I gave him a 'come on now' look. "Hey, you're the one who wanted to do this whole proper, first date business. You can't wimp out now. Spill it, cowboy," I said.

My sass earned me a genuine smile, albeit a small one.

"Did you ever meet him?" I asked.

He finished his beer. "Once, when I was fifteen. It didn't go well. I told him off."

"You had every right to be angry," I said.

"Yeah, well, I gave him a lot of it, right before nine eleven."

I stilled.

He blew out a harsh exhale. "He usually didn't go downtown. He was Upper East Side all the way, but he had a meeting in the North tower at nine o'clock. He arrived twenty minutes early."

We sat there, staring at each other.

"The plane crashed at eight forty-six a.m."

"City," I whispered.

"Six minutes."

I was at a loss for words.

The whole world felt nine eleven. If you were alive, you remembered exactly where you were when you got the news. But that said, I never knew anyone who'd lost someone close to them on that day. Until now.

"I don't want to feed you platitudes," I said.

His clear green eyes darkened. "So, don't."

I thought about my own fatherless life, missing something you've never known.

"I bet the illusion is better," I said.

His brow quirked.

"I never knew who my father was," I went on. "I'll never know. Most likely, he was an alcoholic miscreant, but I have to admit, when I was younger, I'd let myself imagine he was handsome and rich, maybe famous. I had an elaborate fantasy, that someday he'd find out about me and come and rescue me from the dregs of Devil's Peak."

"The perfect Father-King," he said. "As long as he's unknown, the fantasy upholds."

"Exactly."

"I wasn't born with the last name Grangeworth," he said.

"You weren't?"

He shook his head. "It was in my father's will, that's when he finally acknowledged my existence in a public way. He left a sizeable sum for my mom and me, with one stipulation—that I take his last name by my eighteenth birthday. I didn't want to do it, of course. Why should I, when he had denied me his entire life? But it meant the end of my family living paycheck to paycheck. It would give them security. I couldn't deny them that."

Right as he stopped, the servers came and brought us the most sumptuous steak I would have in my life, with wine beyond anything I'd ever experienced. They brought eight sides. I had three bites of two of them.

But as I was riding the high of good eating, Dare's mood was sinking fast.

"You don't know this about me, but I have a few super powers," I said while scooting a bit closer to him. "I can tell if someone's got a crush, even before they know it themselves. I also have the uncanny ability to be able to name any song in under five notes."

A whisper of a grin showed. "Is that right?"

"Oh yeah, want to test me?"

"Maybe later."

I went on. "And I can feel the air."

Two lines formed between his brows. "Come again?"

"I can walk into any room and sense the mood of everyone in it. And, about twenty seconds ago, yours went south, and right-quick too, if I may say."

He had an elbow on the armrest, with his chin cradled in his cupped hand. "Beautiful and perceptive," he said. "You're right, by the way."

"Thank you for sharing all that with me," I said, meaning it. "I get the feeling you don't let a lot of people in."

"That's true," he said as he signaled the server for the bill, then held my gaze, his smile closing and growing tight. "I've had a really good time tonight."

Okay, so what's the problem?

"I did too," I said.

He nodded. "Yeah, that's why this is going to be hard."

"What is?" I asked.

"Me telling you I'm out."

The air stopped flowing to my lungs. Everything burned.

"I don't understand," I said. I felt like I was falling through a different kind of tunnel, one where gravity and weightlessness crashed inside my gut.

"Yeah, sorry Dixie, but there's no way I'm gonna be your sexual guinea pig. Find someone else."

Eight

"But I don't want to go among mad people," Alice remarked.
"Oh, you can't help that," said the Cat:
"we're all mad here. I'm mad. You're mad."
"How do you know I'm mad?" said Alice.
"You must be," said the Cat, "or you wouldn't have come here."
~Lewis Carroll, *Alice in Wonderland*

Dare

I DIDN'T EXPECT it.

I'm not used to people surprising me.

And she just surprised the hell out of me.

Because when I told her I was out, she didn't look like someone whom had been inconvenienced or just had her pride stung.

She was gutted.

And that gave me a flare of hope, one I felt in my center of my chest. Alice may have been insisting she wasn't interested in anything more than a sexual relationship, and only for the purpose of her academic ambition, but her reaction revealed there was more here for her than she admitted.

I pulled her chair right next to mine, draping my arm over the back.

I was now close enough to hear her breath hitch in the back of her throat and see her pupils dilate.

It was time I told her how this was going to go and I hoped like hell she was up for the ride.

"Listen, Alice, I know myself well. There's no way I'm going to be down for some clinical fuck," I said. I could feel the intensity rolling off me in waves as I talked with my hands. "I've got this mental picture in my head, of us tearing into each other, only to have you jot down notes in your lab notebook, scheduling our next session like it's an appointment with the dentist or something."

She let out a sigh of relief. "Is that it? That's your issue?" she asked, her hand over her heart, which only brought my attention to those gorgeous breasts of hers. "City, it wouldn't be like that."

She's not fully getting it.

I grimaced. "I'm not someone who believes in a lot of rules, but I do have two I live by. One, I don't do anything half-assed, and second, I keep the circle of people I trust small. Part of what that means is I don't fuck around. I don't do casual."

Her gaze went from my eyes to my mouth. I wanted to take that mouth. I craved her body in my bed, but I knew myself too well. I was greedy. Just her body would never be enough.

"If you don't do casual, then why did you agree to be part of my study in the first place?" she asked.

I stared.

"Wow, it's always the smart ones who lack common sense."

She scrunched her nose. "Excuse me?"

Totally adorable.

"How do you not get that I've been looking for any 'in' with you I could find?"

She searched my face, as if she were trying to determine if I was for real or full of shit. Right then, I decided I wasn't going to hold anything back, even if it costed me my chance.

"Dixie, how the hell can you say you're studying the psychology of sex and yet you've been hell-bent on only giving your body? Don't you get that great sex happens when all of you is in it? Without the mind and heart, the body can't fully surrender."

"Of course, I get that," she said, barely above a whisper. "It's just that . . ." she blew out a breath. "I'm used to living my life compartmentalized, pieces of me set aside in little boxes. It's how I survived.

"Even when I was with Chad, someone who swore he loved me, I eventually came to realize he only loved the parts of me he could understand or relate to. The rest, he tried to wash away, in ways so small and insidious I didn't even catch on 'til much, much later. I guess I'm still trying to forgive myself for letting him convince me there were pieces of me that weren't good enough."

She looked so small sitting in that big chair next to me.

"I get that. In order to survive, we had to reconfigure ourselves into things not entirely of our creation," I said, reaching out to brush the stray hair out of her eyes. "We've all done it. Just swear to whatever God you believe in to never do it again."

She stared at me.

"What?" I asked.

"How is it I hardly know you, and yet, you get me more than the man I was engaged to?"

"I don't know," I said. And, as I did, I swear I felt my heart come back to life. "But that doesn't make it any less true."

She took my hand into her lap, threading our fingers together.

Her touch already felt like home.

"I can't do half measures," I said.

"I know, but I can't let myself drown in you either. I can't make my life all about your life," she said, squeezing my hand.

"Is that what happened with your ex-fiancé?"

She nodded. "I met him freshman year and we were together

throughout college. We broke up halfway through my master's program, last year. What I thought was my own fairy tale, of the poor girl being swept off her feet by the rich prince of North Carolina, ended up something very different."

I let that sink in. "I'm assuming you're the one who called it off?"

"Yes," she said, picking off an imaginary speck of dust off the skirt of her dress. "Chad didn't take it well. He's used to getting what he wants."

"I bet. You know all the douchebags throughout history are always named either Chad, Dick, Trevor, or Blaine, right?"

Her mouth twitched. "You just made that up. Didn't you?"

I paused, then winked. "I did," I said, "But that doesn't make it any less true."

She busted out laughing.

Warmth spread through me. "Getting you to laugh is going to be my new favorite thing."

Her eyes lit up. "I'll tell you what, City. I wouldn't mind that. Not one bit."

"Challenge accepted." I said. "One more thing."

"Hmm?"

"I want to hear about him. I want to hear *all* your stories," I said. "But first, we're going to leave this restaurant before we close it down and I'm taking you back to my place. We may end up just talking all night or I may find myself dick deep in you. You up for that?"

She sunk her top teeth into her bottom lip. "We're going down the rabbit hole, aren't we?"

"Dixie, you have no idea," I said as I stood up to take her away. "I'm hoping you're going to find that falling's never been such a rush."

"How can you know so soon?" she asked, looking up at me.

"I know because it's going to be with you."

Nine

"It was much pleasanter at home," thought poor Alice, "when one wasn't always growing larger and smaller, and being ordered about by mice and rabbits. I almost wish I hadn't gone down the rabbit-hole—and yet—and yet—..."
~Lewis Carroll, *Alice in Wonderland*

Alice

"YOU *DO* REALIZE you've set up the perfect honey trap," I said.

Dare chuckled to himself. "Is that right?"

I had my heels off and was laying on my stomach in front of his fireplace. He had poured us a couple of whiskeys and started building a fire.

I kept petting the rug underneath me. "It's a good thing I'm a proper carnivorous Southerner by the way," I said, brushing my cheek back and forth. "Because I don't even care that this is an animal skin rug. I swear, laying on this thing is like experiencing the softness of heaven right here on earth."

"Should I leave the two of you alone?"

I narrowed my eyes into playful slits. "Don't tease. Because I think

I may live on this rug patch for the rest of my days," I said, propping my elbows on the rug and resting my chin on the heels of my palms. "Just don't tell me what kind of animal it is, okay? Because then I'm going to picture its cute lil' face and then the whole experience is ruined for me."

His body shook with quiet laughter. "Yeah, if you knew, you wouldn't be happy," he said. He grabbed one of those long-nosed lighters and flicked the switch. "Although, if it's any consolation, it was a gift from an early patron of mine."

My mind started overthinking. "A woman?" I asked.

"Yes," he said, stopping what he was doing to look over at me. Damn, he was so strong and beautiful. "Does that idea make you jealous?"

I let out a sigh. "I know I'm supposed to say 'no,' to feign indifference, but I'm not that built that way."

His nostrils flared. "Good, because I'm not either." He crawled over, his body a panther on the prowl as he flipped me over and his weight settled over mine. My hands immediately went under his shirt, needing to feel his skin, the muscles in his back taut as he hovered over me, gazing down.

"I like you wanting me," he said as I stared up at him. Damn, my heart was pounding hard. I was sure he could feel it. "And I really like feeling your hands on me."

I let my nails scratch down his back, which made his eyes get lazy, a groan humming in the back of his throat. "Shit, Dixie, I'm holding on to my control by a very weak thread."

"Why?" I whispered, my hands sliding down past his waistband, cupping the globes of his perfect ass. "Don't hold back."

The clouds returned. "I don't want to scare you off."

"I don't want that either," I said. "But I promise, I'll tell you if I feel overwhelmed."

He studied me. "I need that, Dixie. I'm decent at reading people too, but I have to know the woman in my bed feels free to tell me anything, even if you're worried I won't like it."

Something was working behind his eyes, his mind going somewhere.

"The same is true for you, City," I said.

He gazed down at me, lines creased between his eyes.

"No holding back?" he asked.

"No holding back," I said.

"Alright," he expelled a breath he seemed to be holding. "Whatever this is, however long it is, I need exclusivity. I don't want another man even thinking for a second he has a shot in there," he said, his eyes darting, searching mine. "Can you give me that?"

As much as I loved groping his ass, I needed my hands to soothe him. I stroked his hair, rested the other hand along the crook of his neck, feeling his pulse racing.

This mattered to him, and, if I was to be honest with myself, it mattered to me too.

"Yes, I can give you that, City," I said. "No other women for you either."

He scoffed. "Please, I haven't been with anyone in over a year," he said.

I felt my jaw drop. "Is that true? How is that true?"

He searched my face. "You haven't heard?"

My brows furrowed. "About what?"

"It's not a 'what,' but a 'who,'" he said.

He must be referring to that girl, Chloe, the one Rayna mentioned.

Dare must've seen a flash of recognition.

"So, you *have* heard," he said, his lips pressed into a thin line.

"Only a name, not what happened," I said. "Hey, we don't need to share all our stories tonight, okay? There's time."

His shoulders dropped. "That sounds good."

"Do I get you now?" I asked.

He broke into a huge smile. "You mean do I get *you* now?"

I opened my mouth to answer, but he had had enough talking. He kissed me, giving my body all his weight, the pressure feeling so good, centering me even as I was soaring. He gave all of himself in his kiss, his tongue playing with mine, his teeth tugging at my bottom lip. Wetness flooded in a delicious way between my legs.

"I-I need you," I moaned as his mouth skimmed my jaw, his whiskers scraping against the skin of my neck and chest. I was on fire.

"Me too, Dixie," he groaned, giving me space so I could unbutton his shirt, him practically ripping it off his arms before he turned me over on my stomach, taking my zipper in between his teeth and working it down.

Holy shit. I felt his mouth at the base of my spine, his tongue and lips working their way up as he slid my dress off my shoulders. He lifted himself off me so I could shimmy the rest away. He was on his knees, straddling my legs, and I turned around to see him unbuckling his belt.

"No," I said, my hands taking over as I turned back onto my back. "That's for me."

I whipped the belt away, then undid his trousers, and he promptly moved his legs to kick them away. He was naked, lying beside me—the picture of rugged virility. He had curls of black chest hair with a trail leading to his generous and long cock, which laid heavy along his hip. He was muscular everywhere, with gorgeous thick thighs, taut abs and strong arms. He had some black curls around his cock, but he must've kept it trimmed because I could still see every part of him.

I was still in my bra and underwear, so I unsnapped the back hooks and slowly let my bra fall away. His lips parted and his cock twitched. Just looking at him, feeling his longing for me amped my need.

"You're beautiful everywhere," he said, reaching over, his arms snaking around my waist, pulling me to him. I was now flush against him, his scent and warmth enveloping us. My nipples were hard points, my breasts heavy and sensitive, sparking desire through my body as they rubbed against the hairs of his broad chest.

"You feel amazing," I said, before he started kissing me again and rubbing his large cock between my legs. I was already slick with arousal and he groaned when he felt it.

"Fuck, Dixie, you're already wet for me."

He was dragging the head of his length right along my center. My head lolled back as I held onto his shoulders, hitching a leg over his hip, grinding in tandem with him.

"I don't want to come yet, but that feels so good," I moaned.

I felt his mouth at my nipples, going back and forth, sucking and flicking my sensitive nubs while moving his hips, creating beautiful friction.

"I'm going to make you come a lot tonight," he said, getting rougher, going faster. "I want to see you fall apart, and I'm going to use my dick, my fingers and my

mouth on you to make it happen."

I couldn't fully form a response with words. He was working delectable magic on my body. I had become only feeling.

"Oh God," I said, my hips moving in time with his, my forehead resting against his. "I'm close. I-I can't—

"You can, honey," he insisted. My eyes were closed, but I could feel him watching me. "You're going to keep rubbing that sweet pussy until you detonate all over my dick. Then I'm going to fuck you deep and eat you raw because I want to see all the different ways that gorgeous face looks when you're falling apart."

His dirty mouth sent me over the edge. I let out a silent scream, a mouth opened with no sound, my body convulsing in sweaty, sweet delirium.

"That's it. Let go," he whispered in my ear, then kissed along my neck, rubbing his whiskers against my skin. I shivered from all the sensations and he hugged me tighter.

I opened my eyes as I came back.

"Hey," he said, voice still rough with desire.

I smiled. "Hey right back at ya," I said.

I let my hand slide down between us, wrapping it around him. My fingertips couldn't even touch, his length was that thick. I started stroking.

"That feels good, but I want in," he groaned.

"I want *you* in."

He reached for his pants and took the condom out of his wallet. No surprise, it was one of those Magnum XL. I watched as he rolled it over himself, the fire flicking light and shadow between us.

I swallowed. "I hope you'll fit," I said, only half kidding.

He blanketed his body over mine, his cock resting between us, on my stomach.

"We'll go slow, okay?" he asked, both his hands gently holding my head.

I nodded.

His eyes never left mine as he moved his hips. I opened my legs, feeling his cock drag until the tip was at my opening. He started off slow, but I was so wet, so ready, that he slid inside. No pain, but it was snug.

Once he could feel I was good, Dare thrusted fully inside. I swear, I felt him in my throat. And I loved it.

"Baby, it's so good," I moaned. "Don't be gentle. I can take it."

"Fuck, you're perfect for me," he said as he growled and pummeled into me. I grabbed his ass, pushing him as deep as he could go, until he rolled us over in one full sweep. I was on top.

"Ride me," he said, his voice rough. "Work my cock with that sweet, tight pussy." He then held on to my ass as I rode him, tilting my hips on the way down so I could get the exact right angle against my swollen clit. With each movement, I felt my need growing again, sparks of pleasure making every nerve in my body come alive and sing. My ample breasts bounced. His torso jacked up, wrapping his arms around me, his mouth finding my nipples, sucking deep, feeling so hungry I felt his groans right between my legs along with his cock. His thighs pressed against my back. I was surrounded by everything Dare. And when he reached down between us and rubbed me in time with our thrusts, that was it.

There was nothing silent this time. Waves of electric pleasure exploded, making me come hard and moan louder and longer than I ever had in my life. City followed right behind me, his moans almost a growl. Even with the condom, I swore I still felt him come, searing and strong.

It was a good thing he was holding me because I felt dizzy, my head becoming feather light, like it wasn't connected to my body any more.

His breath was hot against my chest, coming out in short pants as he tried to catch his breath. He wasn't the only one. I cradled his head in my arms, resting my cheek against his soft, thick hair.

I felt my eyes getting heavy, drifting off, when he got up in a quick motion, holding me by the waist and under my bottom.

"Where are we going?"

"I want you in my bed," he said, walking us through his apartment, the city alight through his wall of floor-to-ceiling windows. It was like watching a swirl of lights, millions of lit dots morphing into sinewy, parallel lines.

I think I was tipsy from the whiskey.

He kicked open his bedroom door and laid me down in the center of the bed holding the condom in place while sliding out of me.

"I'll be right back," he said, giving a quick kiss to my belly before sauntering to the bathroom. Even though he was built like a lumberjack, he moved with a graceful ease. I loved watching his body, with only the moon and city lights coming in. Walking back towards the bed, I noticed he was still mostly erect.

"You keep staring at my dick like that and I'm going to have to fuck you again," he said, unable to keep the grin off his face.

I guffawed. "That's not the deal breaker you think it is," I said, wiping my eyes. "I'm just surprised to see you're almost ready to go again."

He took a knee to the bed and crawled over, and as soon as he laid down I rolled into him. Without hesitation, he enveloped his body around mine. I nestled my face in his neck, breathing in.

He chuckled. "Are you sniffing me?"

I gave a quick nip. "I am. Deal with it," I said, liking how he played with my hair, running his fingers through it. "I like the way you smell."

"Same. You taste like sugar and smell like jasmine and coconut, like I'm on vacation," he said, letting out a soft laugh.

"You know, recent studies are reporting that the apocrine glands hold special promise as the source of smells that might affect interpersonal interactions."

His lips were pressed to the top of my head. I felt them break out in a big smile. "I've been wondering when I was going to get a slice of that hot, geek brain of yours. Continue."

Now it was my turn to smile. I couldn't help it. I liked the fact that he got off on my inner nerd girl.

"Well, all the other glands have uses that have been identified. But the apocrine glands aren't for temperature-managing functions in people, as they are in other animals. They occur in dense concentrations on hands, cheeks, scalp, breast areolas, and wherever we possess body hair—and are only functional after puberty, when we begin searching for mates."

He snorted. "So, are you saying you primarily drawn to me because of my apocrine gland secretions?"

"Not if you keep using the word *secretions*, I won't be," I said while running my palm back and forth over his chest hair, liking how it tickled. "And, for future reference, I also loathe the words *gelatinous*, *moist*, *viscous flaccid* and *yeast*.

He cracked up. "Those *are* truly awful," he said, while tilting my head, looking into my eyes. "Do you have a list of words that turn you on?"

"*You* turn me on. You and that dirty mouth."

"Oh yeah?" he asked through a sly grin.

"Are you kidding? I thought I was going to come just from listening to you."

His eyes searched mine for a couple of seconds. "That reminds me . . . we've gone through this whole evening and we haven't even talked about your case study, the one for Professor Inappropriate."

"My sister would sure agree with that nickname," I said. "And you're right. I can't believe I forgot to bring it up. But now that you have, what do you want to know?"

He shrugged, rolling onto his back, elbows out and hands cushioning his head. "I don't know. I guess I'm curious what it entails."

"Well, I'm supposed to keep a written record of our relationship. You aren't required to, but if you wanted to keep a log, it's certainly encouraged."

"I guess I can do that. What else?" he asked.

I rolled onto my stomach, propping myself up on my elbows. "Well, he'd love it if we had one of the major categories of sexual dysfunction, but I'm thinking we're going to disappoint the hell out of him, if tonight's any indication."

"True, but I imagine a lot of couples start off hot and heavy, with issues coming up later."

"Yeah, I wouldn't know. I've only ever had one serious relationship and my desire for him lessened because I realized he was an entitled ass, not because of some psycho-biological malady. And growing up, I didn't exactly have models of sexually healthy relationships. What about you?"

He scrubbed his hand over his face. "I don't think she ever got over my father," he said, staring out at nothing in particular. "She dated after him, but I rarely saw the same guy come around more than twice. She says she got her one great love and the rest were just someone to go to dinner with, but I never bought that."

"That's kind of sad," I said.

He grimaced. "Yeah, well, for some, the heart is a resilient muscle, but for others, when their heart breaks, they're eviscerated and they just don't have it in them to put the pieces back together. That's my mom. It wasn't about getting over the man. It was about not getting over the hurt. She never trusted any man after that and she certainly drilled it into my head to not be an asshole, especially to women."

"It sounds like they're one and the same," I said, staring off. "I had to take this upper level bio class in undergrad where the professor showed us a cadaver's heart. Inside were all these tiny tendons. They looked like heart strings. He said it's not uncommon for these tendons to break, especially after a deep emotional trauma. Enough of them break and the heart loses form and is unable to pump blood the way it needs to, leading to heart failure. It's called broken heart syndrome."

He didn't say anything for a while.

Eventually, his eyes found mine in the dark. "All the more reason why I'm glad I let what you said when we first met sink in."

I drew a blank. "What did I say?"

"About me being an asshole, saying either I was always one or had become one. That I had shown you my true colors."

Ah, now I remember.

"Well, I like you *now*," I said, patting his chest.

He laughed. "Well, I hope so," he said, grabbing my wrist and pulling me over him. I laid on top, skin to skin. "I'm realizing something."

"What's that?" I asked.

"I never got dessert tonight," he said, his cock growing hard between us. "And I'm still hungry."

"Oh my God, you're kidding, right? I'm still so full," I said.

He stilled. "Not that kind of hungry, Dixie."

I barely got the "oh" out when he grabbed hold under my arms and hoisted me forward and up, so I was straddling his face.

"Now, feed me what we both need."

It was a request I was happy to oblige.

Needless to say, I didn't get much sleep that night.

Jen

> This piece of rudeness was more than Alice could bear:
> she got up in great disgust, and walked off;
> the Dormouse fell asleep instantly,
> and neither of the others took the least notice of her going,
> though she looked back once or twice,
> half hoping that they would call after her . . .
> ~Lewis Carroll, *Alice in Wonderland*

Dare

LIKE CLOCKWORK, I'M always up with the sun. No matter what. I could be sick. I could have stayed up most of the previous night.

Doesn't matter.

At one point, I even had black-out curtains put in my bedroom, hoping I could fool my Pavlovian brain into getting the rest my body needed.

It didn't work. Neither did pills, booze, weed. So, I gave them up as forms of self-medication a long time ago.

Of course, my ma said my early rising was God's hint to get my lazy ass out of bed and back to church. She was Italian Catholic and went three times a week. She said the extra visits were meant to compensate for my piss poor lack of attendance.

Yeah, she's a pistol.

My building faced east, which meant I was able to attend my own version of church every day and bask in God's glory, each rising sun a unique creation that I could fool myself into feeling was just for me.

This morning was another beauty, but this time it was the brunette with the big blue eyes sleeping next to me, taking all my attention. Her long, thick hair was splayed across the white pillows, as she slept on her back. The sheets were at her waist, so I was treated to watching her beautiful, bare breasts slowly rise and fall with her soft snore.

"Alice . . . Alice?"

"Hmm?" she mumbled, still half asleep.

"Want to sleep in or come down to the studio with me?"

She turned, mushing her face into the pillow. "If you are a sadist, you should've told me that from the get go. This is wicked early."

That made me laugh. "Then sleep, baby. I'll make some coffee. Come down when you're ready. It's the third floor."

She grunted and nodded.

I made myself a big mug and took the elevator down to my studio. I was surprised to see Ingrid already there. She also wasn't a big fan of early mornings.

"Is it the end of days or something?" I asked, being a smartass.

"Good morning to you too, sunshine," she said, not taking her eyes off her work, paintbrush in hand, the same piece from the other day. "And I'm the only one who can make Book of Revelations jokes around here."

"That's fair," I said, taking a sip of coffee. "So, what's up?"

She frowned. "I have the group show at Sean Kelly at the end of the month, remember?"

"Of course, I do, 'grid," I said smiling down at her, trying not crack a smile at the sight of her. That blue hair of hers was all over the place and she was wearing her favorite unicorn onesie. Yeah, the kind with the pajama feet and the flap in the back, just like they make for little kids.

"Didn't Petra already choose the pieces she wanted for the show?" I asked. Petra was in charge of curating group exhibitions for Sean Kelly Gallery.

She tossed the brush down, fisting her hair with both hands.

"Yeah, but I don't know. I think I should give her a few more choices, don't you think?"

The show was her first big break, and I knew it meant a lot to her. Sean Kelly was one of the most influential galleries in the New York art scene, representing big name artists such as Marina Abramovi and Mariko Mori. This show was something she'd earned all on her own, outside my influence. As close as we were, I couldn't blame her for wanting something of her own. I was like the big brother with an even bigger shadow.

"Do what you've got to do, but don't make yourself sick over it," I said.

Behind me I heard, "Well, I haven't seen the others, but the one you're working on is truly compelling."

I knew that voice.

I turned around and there was Alice, coffee in hand, wearing her clothes from last night. Just seeing her made something inside me instantly lighter.

I beamed. "Morning, baby."

She smiled wide. "Hey you." She gave a half wave to Ingrid. "Hi, I'm Alice. We sort of met at your party."

"My bad," I said. "Alice, this is Ingrid. Ingrid, this is Alice."

"Oh great, another Chloe," Ingrid murmured, but loud enough for her to hear.

Alice's face paled, lips parted.

"She's nothing like Chloe, 'grid, and it's completely uncool of you to make that comparison."

She ignored me and focused on Alice.

"Thanks for the art critique, Peggy Sue, but I think I'll pass on valuing the opinion of someone who probably took her cousin to prom."

Wow, that was bitchy, even for her. "Ingrid, what the hell?"

"What? She can't speak for herself?" she asked still scowling. "Let me guess. You're from a small town in the middle of nowhere, you're new to the city, and you're hoping for your big break in something artistic. Am I close?"

I walked over to Alice, standing between them.

"Congratulations, Ingrid, you've just described most of the people in the city who live below Houston," I said, giving her a death stare.

Meanwhile, to her credit, Alice was just sipping her coffee, her shoulder leaning against one of the pillars, watching the show.

"Are you this threatened by every woman in City's life?" she asked.

Ingrid's jaw moved side to side. "City?"

"It's a nickname, 'grid," I said, crossing my arms.

Alice stepped forward. "Well, you got two out of three. I *am* from a small town in North Carolina. In fact, it's so tiny, I don't think even Google Earth could find it. And while I am new to town, I'm here for grad school—not to star in my own Fame movie remake," she said. "Listen, Ingrid, I don't know you, and stereotypes aside, you certainly don't know me either. I appreciate you have your own relationship with Dare and I'm not looking to get in the way of that. So, maybe we can start over?"

She walked closer to us. "It's not that, Alice. He's like my brother and nothing's going to change that," she said while shoving her hands in her pockets. "I don't know what he told you about Chloe . . ."

I interrupted. "We haven't gotten to that part of our scheduled programming, kiddo," I said.

Ingrid's eyes rounded. "She hasn't Googled you or heard from her friends?"

"No, I haven't," Alice said. "And I can't promise someone won't slip, but I'm certainly not going to ask. I'm curious as hell, but I'll wait 'til Dare's ready. I know what it's like when people think they know all about you from stories they hear."

"Holy shit, you're like a unicorn," Ingrid mumbled under her breath.

I gave Ingrid's arm a playful back slap. "I know, right?"

We must've been staring because Alice shook her head. "It's like suddenly *I'm* part of the exhibit," she said, looking at her phone for the time. "Listen, this has been a certain kind of entertaining, but I've got to go. I just came down here to say goodbye."

"You and I are going to talk about this later," I muttered to Ingrid before following Alice through the studio.

As soon as we were in the elevator, I said, "Hey, I'm sorry about that. Ingrid's actually a really good kid, salt-of-the-earth."

She smiled. "I'm not upset about Ingrid," she said. "It's obvious she's very protective of you. It's also obvious there's nothing sexual there for either of you. In time, she'll mature and learn to be more . . . nuanced . . . when trying to assess people."

I studied her, to make sure she was really alright.

She really was.

I smiled, shaking my head. "Sorry, I'm not used to such a level-headed approach. The art world tends to attract a lot of drama."

"We attract what we are, City," she said, sporting a wry grin.

Smart-ass. "Are you trying to say I'm the drama magnet?"

"No," she said. "*You* just did."

I crossed my arms. "Is this what it's going to be like, to date a shrink in training?"

Her smile fell.

Shit, that sounded harsher than I intended.

"Hey, I didn't mean it that way," I said, reaching for her. She softened, letting me take her hand. I buried my face in her neck. "You still smell like me."

"I do?"

"Oh yeah," I said, rubbing my nose and mouth against her skin.

"You smell like me, too. I like it," she said, her voice coming out breathy. "I like the idea of marking you and you marking me, part of an array of some darker fantasies I have."

Fuck, she's perfect for me. I swallowed the lump in my throat.

We walked out of the elevator, but she seemed in a rush now.

"I've got brunch with the girls," she said, getting shy on me, not meeting my eye.

What the hell? "Wait, what just happened, baby?"

She gave a forced smile. "Nothing. I'm all kinds of good." She leaned in and gave a quick kiss. "I don't like to be late is all."

I didn't say anything. I certainly didn't believe a word she just said, but something had spooked her. "You know where to find me," I said, unlocking the front door and holding it open.

I got another tight smile. And then, she was gone.

Eleven

**"You don't know much,' said the Duchess; ' and that's a fact."
~Lewis Carroll, *Alice's Adventures in Wonderland***

Alice

"IF I HAD spent the whole night sampling the delectable man buffet that is Dare Grangeworth, y'all would've been on the receiving end of a 'see you later' text, that's for sure," Caroline said, dropping a sugar cube in her tea.

Rayna nodded. "Seriously, chica, we would've understood. Right, Lulu?"

Lulu startled, lost in her thoughts. "Oh! Yes, of course we would've understood. It's not like our Sunday brunches are mandatory."

I shrugged. "I know, I know. Did you ever consider I just wanted to hang with y'all? If it weren't for this little ritual, we could go weeks without checking in. We're all so busy."

"Oh poo, was he a possum in the sack? Did he not know basic geography?" Caroline asked, keeping her voice low.

Both Lulu and Rayna cracked up.

"Your Southern expressions kill me," Rayna said, shaking her head.

"What does that mean?" Lulu asked, leaning close.

I rolled my eyes. "She's asking if he is either playing dead in bed or doesn't know where the clitoris is," I informed them. "And to answer your question, that's not the issue. He's exceptional in bed and it was only our first time."

"That bodes well," Lulu smiled over her teacup.

"So, what's the issue?" my sister asked.

I looked over. "What? There isn't an issue."

Caroline gave a 'don't BS me' look.

"It's new," I said. "Aren't you always the one who says 'let them miss you some'?"

"You *do* say that," Lulu smiled while giving me a little wink. "And I, for one, appreciate your application of classic gaming and economic theory onto social, interpersonal relationships."

I may have let a giggle slip.

Caroline let out an exasperated sigh. "*Fine.* You just want some girl time. That's your story and you're sticking with it."

"Thank you kindly," I said, high fiving myself on the inside.

"For someone who's working so dang hard to be a head peeper someday, you'd think you'd want to address your own bullshit head on. Because sister, you've got more issues than a doctor's office waiting room."

I could feel the crooked smile on my face.

I pointed my fork in her direction. "And you need to work on your tell," I said. "I always know when sister is ticked because the Carolina in her comes out real strong."

"Hmph."

"You know, we are sitting on some prime-time, juicy tidbits that aren't even being touched," I said, redirecting.

"It's true," Lulu said while wiggling in her seat. "I'm on a happy giggle loop and I don't want it to ever end."

"That's so awesome," I said, with everyone agreeing.

"What's going on?" Rayna asked.

She threaded her white blond hair behind her ears, her grey eyes shining. "I just got the early reviews of my first product rollout through Beck's company."

"Remind me, what did you decide to release first?" Rayna asked before taking a bite of her omelet.

"The hot solar cells?" Lulu answered, barely able to contain her excitement. "That's the one that'll convert heat into concentrated beams of light, giving people worldwide a cheap and continuous power source."

"That's right," Rayna nodded.

"That's huge," I said.

"I know!" Lulu was beaming. "So far, we've heard from Consumer Reports, M.I.T. Tech Reviews, Scientific American magazine, BigThink . . . they're saying Hot Dots—that's the name Beck and I came up with—may be one of the game changers of the twenty-first century."

I reached out for her, giving her hand a squeeze. The others followed.

"We are beyond happy for you," I said, my smile so big it was ready to split my head open.

"Yeah, there's only one problem," she said, the sadness coming in like rain clouds.

"If you're talking about that good-for-nothing family of yours, I don't want you worrying about a thing," Rayna said, squaring her shoulders. "I'm going to introduce you to my financial advisor. Phillipa's a genius. And I'm also going to hook you up with my attorney. If there's such a thing as a shark with a heart of gold, it's Marie. If they even *think* of harassing you, I have friends at the tenth precinct who will be more than happy to pay those *puntas* a visit."

We were all protective of Lulu, but it was fair to say Rayna registered higher on that particular Richter scale than the rest of us. Maybe because she was inherently maternal or perhaps because her younger brother, Mario, was also on the Autism spectrum, like Lulu.

"Okay, then maybe I have another problem," she said, picking at her eyebrows.

"Stop that," Caroline said, gently taking her hand in hers. "Last time you picked out all your eyebrow hairs, it took forever for them to grow back. Remember?"

Lulu nodded, frowning.

"So, what else is wrong?" I asked.

She huffed, closing her eyes for a few seconds before opening them and saying. "I think I'm in love with Beck and he has no idea. But I'm sure if he did, I'd just make him feel uncomfortable, at best. At worst, he wouldn't want to work with me anymore."

We all stared. Lulu had never admitted to having feelings for anyone. In fact, she had always viewed romantic relationships as a waste of time and regarded her sexual needs like an errand on a check list, something to take care of with her vibrator or with a couple of friends with bennies she had panting after her.

So her not-so-little declaration, was big. Huge.

"We're going to help you," Rayna said, a steely determination in her eyes.

"Of course, whatever you need," I said, with Caroline nodding like a bobble head.

"I don't know how to flirt," she sighed. "I don't know how to do small talk. I don't know how to do any of it."

Rayna's phone rang. When she saw the name, her nostrils flared and her mouth tightened. "We've got you, Lulu, but I need to take this."

"Who is it?" I asked.

"Not important, but if this man says what I *think* he's going to say? It's off with his head!" she said while dragging her finger across her throat and getting up from the table. "Hello, Captain Tight Ass . . ."

"What was that about?" I asked.

Caroline leaned in, so only we could hear. "I haven't gotten the whole story, but it's something to do with Mario. Wrong place, wrong time sort of thing. She's beside herself."

"Why hasn't she said anything to the rest of us?" I asked.

I had to admit I was a little hurt.

Caroline shook her head. "Please. I wasn't supposed to know either. I just happened to be in her apartment when she got a call about it the other day. You know how weirdly protective she gets when it comes to her brother."

"Alright, let's take care of brunch for her," I said. "Lord knows she's covered for us plenty of times."

We all scattered after we paid the bill. At first, I went to the New York Public Library to study, but it was too crowded. Then, I went to my university's library and it was too quiet. So I went home and got a little work done, but I couldn't pinpoint it. I felt restless and was only able to focus in short spurts.

Otherwise, I was in a kind of fog. But the haze cleared and it finally hit me why I had left him in such a rush.

I had gotten spooked, not by him this time, but of me.

What did it mean that I liked the idea of him marking me? Was some ancient, prehistoric section of my brain taking control over my rational, civilized self? I had lived for so long in my prefrontal cortex, with logic and executive functioning happily in charge, ensuring I was organized and analytical, making safe choices. But I had gotten a hint of something raw, primordial and hungry when I wanted him to mark me with his gaze, his teeth, his seed. My limbic brain wasn't just fight or flight, not just there to let me know that my body was experiencing an orgasm. She was my instinctive self, my animal urges and she wanted to be marked. She wanted to be claimed, not out of weakness, but out of desire and her own virility.

I had no idea who that part of me was, but I was opened to finding out.

I grabbed one of my smaller duffle bags and packed it with enough stuff for several days. Along with my school backpack, I took my stuff and walked out of my place.

I took my time, strolling through Chelsea, going southeast towards Greenwich Village, one of my favorite neighborhoods in the city. The stuff I was carrying was heavy, but I didn't mind the burden. The weight was grounding, a needed juxtaposition to the lightheadedness I was experiencing.

Both heavy and light battled inside my body until eventually, I got tired and hailed a cab, giving cross streets I had just learned. I paid the fare, stopped when I got to the sidewalk and stood in front of a building. I was there for a while, long enough for the sun to be going down.

Until I heard a door unlatch and open.

And there he was.

Our eyes locked.

"It's about time," he said, his voice barely above a whisper.

But it was enough. It was everything.

I walked straight into his arms as he bent into me, my nose pressed into the middle of his chest.

And without a word, he took all that I carried, along with my hand in his, and brought me in from the cold.

Twelve

"The rabbit-hole went straight on like a tunnel
for some way, and then dipped suddenly down,
so suddenly that Alice had not a moment to think about stopping
herself before she found herself falling down a very deep well."
~Lewis Carroll, *Alice's Adventures in Wonderland*

Dare

I WAS STANDING in my bathroom, scratching the underside of my jaw as I surveyed the utter lack of counter space left in my bathroom. Alice had been at my place for less than forty-eight hours—and frankly, she had fought me on the extra day—but I pleaded my case with my mouth between her legs, so that worked.

And I'm also guessing I made her feel comfortable enough for her to unfurl all the products in her arsenal.

"Babe, you barely wear any make-up," I called out. "How is it possible you have this much shit?"

She was still in my bed, wrapped in a cocoon of sheets and blankets.

"Says the man who wakes up looking like something off a billboard."

"I'm just saying, you don't need all this crap."

She mumbled something I couldn't hear and may have shot me the bird before her hand snuck back under the covers. I shook my head and let out a soft laugh.

Every man bitches about all the stuff their girlfriends or wives keep around, but what the hell was the point of having space if not for your woman to feel at home? Besides, if a guy has a shit ton of crap for his hair or subscribes to a skin regimen, he needs to double check his man card. He was even more of a pussy if he acted like buying a box of tampons was the equivalent of getting his balls cut off.

That said, I wasn't above giving her shit.

I finished up in the bathroom. "How is it possible there's any hair left on your head?"

"Cute, but newsflash City—you're barking up the wrong tree if you waiting on me to agree with you."

I kept going. I was having too much fun. "By the way, I cleaned out your brush. It was time to set that furry pet free."

I saw one blue eye peeking from inside her long mane—and it looked angry. "And to think, I was all ready to give you a morning blow job. That is, until you sassed me."

Ah shit. "Now, wait a sec," I said, crawling back in bed. "Let's not be hasty."

"Nope, forget it," she laughed, shaking her head. "It's too bad, too, because I'm really good at it."

I've had Alice in a variety of ways, but haven't yet gotten to see that perfect mouth around my dick. Maybe because I couldn't seem to get enough of her taste. I'd catch a hint of her scent, like a feral dog, and that was it—I needed my mouth in there.

"Actually, Ms. Leighton, I think this aforementioned promise of exceptional fellatio is a prime example of the kind of critical data points necessary for my case study notes, to be as useful as possible, in the name of science, of course."

"Oh, of course," she said, playing along. "That's very considerate of you, Mr. Grangeworth, thinking of the best ways to benefit science."

"I know. I'm a giver," I said as I pulled her close, noticing she had on a tight tee and underwear. "Hey, didn't we both fall asleep naked last night?"

She pushed her hair away from her face. "No, I waited until *you* fell asleep, then got some stuff out of my bag to put on."

I squeeze that luscious ass of hers.

"Care to share why? I like having full access, Dixie."

"I don't like sleeping naked. Never have. Besides, it's good for you to have to work for it," she said, biting her bottom lip, looking up at me through those long lashes.

This woman is going to kill me.

"I don't know about that. Feels like you're creating unnecessary barriers towards intimacy. I'm going to have to write about this in my case study journal and process my emotions," I teased. This was one of my new lines I liked to use, usually if I wasn't getting my way.

"Yeah, I've got something for you to process," she said, a wicked gleam in her eye before going back under the comforter. I was just about to protest, until I felt her hot, wet mouth wrap around me. That shut me right up.

"Mmm, I knew you'd taste good," she said, continuing to hum as her lips and tongue worked my tip. I ripped the covers off because there was no way I was missing this show.

She crawled over and perched right between my legs, those cerulean eyes locked on mine as she worked her way down my shaft, one hand stroking in time with her mouth while the other lightly tickled my balls.

"Ah hell, that feels amazing," I groaned, my eyes ready to roll to the back of my head, but not wanting to miss a second of her working me. My hips couldn't help but thrust forward as she picked up speed, her hums vibrating up and down my spine.

"Fuck Dixie, that's it. Suck me. Yeah, don't be gentle. Yank it too."

My head lulled back as I fisted the sheets.

But then I felt her squirm and I opened my eyes to see her hand reaching between her legs. *Holy shit, that's the hottest thing ever.*

I let her play with herself for a few beats before I jackknifed up, grabbing her by the hips and pivoting her around, then moving her panties aside, so I had her sweetness in my mouth while she continue to suck and pull on my cock.

She wasn't gentle with me and I sure wasn't going easy on her. I savored her heat on my face, as I flicked her hard and fast with my tongue. She moaned and started grinding into my mouth as I held onto her ass. My girl was so wet and needy, and I was this close to coming down her throat. But I wanted her there with me. Gently, as I lapped her up, I worked a finger inside her puckered opening, using her arousal to ease my way in.

Her moans became wild, as I fucked her ass while she used my mouth to get herself off. I loved every second of it.

She was keening. "Holy shit, that's it . . . yeah, fuck me hard. I can take it. I love it like that. That's it, I'm going to come. I'm—I'm . . ."

Hearing her like that, using my mouth, made liquid fire shoot down my spine. Every muscle in my body tensed as I let it all go. There was an explosion of neon light and color behind my eyelids, blasting like fireworks and melting into a warm haze.

She took my release down her throat, cleaning me off with her tongue.

I could watch her do that all day.

Every time with Alice just kept getting better.

"I might have brain damage after that," I said, catching my breath.

She smiled, her eyes closed, with her tits pressed into my stomach, giving me all her weight as I stroked her ass and the back of her legs. I loved everything about her body.

"I think you sucked the life out of me," I said, my voice hoarse.

She chuckled, but didn't move. "That's only fair. I'm totally dead right now. It's official. You killed me."

"Death by orgasm?"

She looked up, but only one eye opened. "Death by the orgasm of my life. Jesus, Dare, that mouth of yours missed its calling."

"Don't even joke," I said as I moved us so we were both laying on our sides, facing one another. "When I was first starting out, you have no idea how easy it could have been."

"How easy *what* could have been?"

"To have sold myself while trying to sell my work," I said, but seeing the concern in her eyes, I added, "Hey, it didn't happen, so no worries. But it's more common than you think."

"I'm sure it is. This isn't an easy city to survive in," she sighed. "One minute I'm feeling ten feet tall and confident, and the next, like I'm almost invisible."

"Do you miss it, the South?" I asked.

"It'll always be part of me, but being anonymous is such a relief in a lot of ways, especially after living in a small town almost all my life. People would ask me how my mama was, slopping sugar all over, and then talk trash behind her back. I was afraid to do anything, for fear people would say, 'like mama, like daughter'.

"Then I got to Chapel Hill and Chad and I were immediately a thing. He's high cotton—that means he's from a very wealthy Southern family. They all had a mind to grooming me into something above my raisin'. So, totally different circumstances, and yet, still living under a microscope."

I was listening, my fingers making lazy circles on the curve of her hip. I liked listening to her talk, hearing her Southern lilt. I traced her tiny freckles. She had them in a smattering across her lower back and there were a few right along her hip, the ones I was enjoying now.

She watched my fingers. "I had a blind lover once, who told me those little raised freckles actually spelled out the word 'freaky' in Braille."

"Get the fuck out of here," I said. "Is that true?"

She nodded. "No," she said with a straight face before cracking up.

"Are you shitting me?"

She rolled on her back, still laughing. "I had you there, for, like, a few seconds. Admit it!"

I tried to look pissed, but I couldn't keep my game face straight. So, I tickled her until she screamed, and she was only saved by her alarm going off.

"Time for school, little one," I said. "I know we showered last night, but—

"Yeah, we need another one," she said, walking to the bathroom as I watched her gorgeous, full ass move towards the shower. She stopped, staring at the contraption, scrunching her nose.

"I have no idea how to turn this thing on," she said, her frustration obvious. "I know I should be able to figure it out, but in my life I've never seen a shower this fancy. Even Chad's people didn't have something like this."

I stroked her back. "Hey, stop being so hard on yourself. It took a guy three days just to get the shower heads right. That's not including the rest that needed to get done," I said, pointing to the buttons, sharing the sequence if she wanted to adjust. "But it's also voice activated, so just tell it what you want. I'm thinking you'll be good at bossing it around."

She gave a pretend glare but then kissed me, letting out a sigh.

"Sorry, I was being silly."

"You're not being silly," I reassured her. "I think the thing was designed by a former NASA engineer, so don't take it personally."

I pulled her under the water, pumped some of her shampoo into my hands and started washing her hair.

"I love having my hair washed," she moaned, her head back, eye closed, letting me help her relax.

"Good," I said, giving her a deep scalp massage, liking how she leaned into my touch. "You know, before I was a Grangeworth, I was a DeMarco," I told her as I worked up the lather.

"That was your last name before?"

"Yeah, feels like another life," I said. "Being a DeMarco was simpler in a lot of ways. I didn't live large, but we always had plenty to eat and a roof over our head. My ma and I lived with my grandparents, who are still alive and both total pissers by the way."

"Pissers?" she asked.

"Ball busters, but in a good way," I said. "It's a compliment in Brooklyn." I rinsed her hair and proceeded with the conditioner.

I kept talking. "But everything I owned, until I was fifteen, was a hand-me-down. My kicks were off-brand because there was no way I was going to ask for the real thing when they killed themselves to send me to private school until I got into Bronx Science.

"Then suddenly, I'm a Grangeworth, and his widow—God bless her because it couldn't have been easy—finds out about me and takes it upon herself to show me how the other half lives. To give me what her man should've done. But if you don't think I wasn't shitting bricks every time I sat at a dinner with ten friggin' forks in my face, you're wrong. Or when my career first took off, I had clients who would hand me the wine list and ask me to pick what I thought would go best with the sturgeon or whatever . . . do you get what I'm saying?"

I helped her rinse out the conditioner and started soaping myself up. She wiped the water out of her eyes and gave me a sweet little smile, nodding.

"I do. I hear you. Just an FYI, I can be really hard on myself."

We're going to work on that, as soon as I figure out how to stop doing the same thing.

I smiled as I watched her working that soap—and me—into a lather as she washed her thighs, in between her legs, taking extra time on her breasts. By the time I met her eye, I saw that impish gleam.

"You're enjoying fucking with me, Dixie?"

"Oh, I am *soooo* enjoying fucking with you, City," she said. "And if I didn't have to meet with my advisor in about an hour, I'd fuck with you some more."

We finished up, drying off. "What's the rest of your day?" I asked.

She did that wrapping-turban thing with the towel around her head. "After I meet with my advisor, I have another sesh with Professor Inappropriate. Caroline is in love with your nickname for him, by the way. Then I have a lot of reading to get through. You?"

"I've got a solo show opening around the holidays. I'll be ass-deep in that today. Plus, I need to have a quick meeting with Ingrid."

"Everything okay?" she asked, her eyes tentative.

"Yeah, it's standard stuff," I lied. "She runs the studio spaces and the gallery downstairs." Well, that part was true.

She blew out her hair, did what she did to be even more gorgeous while I threw on my standard jeans and a T-shirt, followed by making her coffee to take with her. I texted my driver and sparring partner, Omar (he's a former light weight boxer), to be ready to take her to the university.

When I looked up, Alice was ready to go, with her small duffle by her feet. And she looked nervous.

"I don't know how to say this, so I'll just say it. I can't stay here anymore."

Thirteen

Either the well was very deep, or she fell very slowly, for she had plenty of time as she went down to look about her and to wonder . . .
~Lewis Carroll, *Alice's Adventures in Wonderland*

Alice

I REALLY NEED to work on my word choices and delivery.

"Say again?" he asked, his coffee cup stopping in mid-air.

"Oh my God, that's not what I meant!" I said, walking fast over to him. "I didn't phrase that right."

He put the cup down, both brows raised.

"I love staying here, but it's important that I have some time that's just mine," I said, my hands snaking around his muscled torso while I gazed up at him. I wondered if I'd ever be able to get over how masculine and stunning he was. "It would be easy—*too easy*—to meld my life into yours, without bothering to make something that was my own. I've only been here for a couple of months."

His expression relaxed, one of his arms draping around me.

"That's fine, but you *do* realize you already have your own life, right?"

I shrugged. "Well, the start of one," I said.

His mouth quirked. "Alice, you've been here the equivalent of a half minute and already you're settling into grad school, got a half decent place to live, and your own crew. Most people who come to the city? It takes them years to find what you already have."

I grimaced. "Most of that is my sister's doing. She did all the heavy lifting."

"Dixie, this can be a place where everyone is out for themselves," he said, cupping my face in his hands, which always made my belly flutter. "So, whether it's from your sister or me or whoever, someone offers you help—assuming it's not some fucker—you take it."

His phone beeped from an incoming text. He eyed the screen. "Alright, Omar's downstairs," he said, grabbing both my bags and walking us to the elevator. "Do your thing, but I want you back here, in my bed, by the weekend at the latest."

We got in the elevator and I noticed he was suppressing a grin.

"What?" I asked.

He shook his head. "Uh no, it'll only piss you off."

The elevator dinged and he gestured for me to exit first.

"C'mon, you can't do that," I said, bumping him with my shoulder as we walked to the waiting car. "I promise, I won't get mad."

He guffawed. "I'm not falling for that trap, honey," he said as he opened the front door of the gallery, giving Omar a quick, half wave.

"Have a productive day, Dixie," he winked.

I used my body to block him from the car door handle.

I crossed my arms and arched a brow.

He didn't hesitate, getting right in my space, our bodies barely touching. My nipples pebbled under my shirt, just having him close.

But he didn't have to know that. So, I craned my head up and squared my shoulders. He tried not to laugh. I narrowed my gaze.

His bit the corner of his bottom lip, as he bent down and let his lips brush against the shell of my ear. I shivered, his warm breath on my neck.

So much for tough-girl game.

"Later on, when you find yourself craving my mouth and my dick, and touching yourself isn't giving you the relief that little body needs, I don't want you to let pride get in the way of coming back to me sooner than you expected."

"Wow, someone's sure of himself," I mumbled, moving out of the way. He opened my car door. I folded myself in. He placed my bags near my feet.

"I *am* sure. You want to know why?"

I gave him my best stink eye.

His eyes locked with mine. "Because I'm going to be feeling the exact same way. Nothing but you is going to relieve that ache."

My lips parted, the blood in my veins turning into my favorite drug, making me high.

"You are?" I whispered.

He sucked in the air. "Oh yeah, I'm falling fast, right along with you."

HIS OFFICE SMELLED like Vicks vapor rub and clove cigarettes.

I didn't even know they still *made* clove cigarettes.

I was also guessing he was living under the assumption that the university's no-smoking policy didn't apply to him.

Must be nice to be a white, entitled and tenured male.

Whatever. I was in his world for now. At least he wasn't smoking. I'd heard he liked to light up and blows smoke rings at students he found irritating.

He coughed, then pounded on the middle of his chest a couple of times as he sat across from me. Most of the baby boomers I knew didn't look their age. The generation known for never trusting anyone over thirty had redefined aging, most looking like they were permanently in their forties or fifties.

Not so for Professor Bails. He looked ninety and sounded like a walking death rattle.

He had my case study journal, my paper outline, and the question-naire I had to fill out to gain admittance into his seminar on his lap. He also had an ancient cassette recorder on the table between us, which he used instead of transcribing notes by hand. After hitting record and in-troducing me, he was finally ready.

"So, this is our second session, Ms. Leighton. I've had a chance to review your case study notes and then re-read your entrance questionnaire. Can you tell me why I would do that?"

"You're doing an informal comparative analysis, trying to determine if there are any psychosexual patterns or proclivities surfacing," I said, reminding myself to breathe. He actually was a lovely man, but I was still nervous.

He offered a warm smile with a nod. "Yes, exactly," he said, then clearing his throat. "You know, one of the reasons why I accepted you, a first year, into my seminar was because I was fascinated by how few partners you've had and by the lack of experimentation."

Silly me, I thought it was because I was one of the top students graduating from my master's program.

"Oh, okay. I wouldn't have guessed that," I blurted out, sounding like someone who couldn't find my ass with both hands in my back pockets.

"It's not a criticism, Ms. Leighton." He was quick to try and reassure me. "It's atypical, but nothing I'm concerned about, per se. Do you have any insight you'd like to share?"

I'd like to share a slap upside your head, you old goat.

Why did I push so hard to be in his seminar again?

"Well, I've always thought iconic social theorist, Cher Horowitz, had the

right idea. When questioned about the same personal anomaly, she stated "I'm not a prude. I'm just highly selective. You see how picky I am about my shoes, and those only go on my feet.'"

The man's mouth actually fell open, like an unhinged barn door.

Serves him right. Besides, Cher from Clueless rocks.

"I'm not familiar with her work," he said. "Perhaps you can bring by some of her publications? I like to stay current, if I can."

I almost felt bad for sassing him. Almost.

"Sure thing."

"Go on, you were saying," he said, scooting his chair forward.

I shrugged. "You've read my profile, so you and I both know my penchant for limited sexual partners and experiences derives from having a mother who has high thresholds for both. Add in some classic daddy abandonment issues, and I was destined to either be the way I am or working a pole."

He had his elbow on the arm rest and cradled his head on his thumb and forefinger. "And you know I had no issue with either directive, as long as they're conscious choices which serve your development and actualization. But I am taking note that yours is a more reactionary pattern. You also tend to gravitate towards men who are older and already established. Again, you like what you like, as one does."

I smiled, not knowing what to say.

"It also seems you and your current partner are sexually compatible?"

Oh yeah, you could say that.

"Yes, we are. Very much so," I said, my thighs clenching at the memory.

"Good. Wonderful!" he said. "Then, my directive for you, over the next couple of weeks, will be to discuss each other's sexual histories and determine if there's something you two want to explore together. Is this an open relationship or monogamous?"

"Monogamous," I said.

"Fine. I also want you to delve into your sexual fantasies, at your speed and comfort level, to determine if there are any you want to explore individually or with your partner."

I jotted down some notes: share sex histories, fantasies.

"Sure beats algebra homework," I muttered to myself.

He laughed. "I'm sure," he said, hitting the stop button. "I'll see you in two weeks. And remember . . ."

I was already up, hoisting my bag over my shoulder. "Yes, professor?"

He handed me back my case study journal. "I don't care what you do or with whom, but I want to see you outside your comfort zone. In fact, I'm going to insist on it."

Fourteen

"Who am I then? Tell me that first, and then, if I like being that person, I'll
come up: if not, I'll stay down here till I'm somebody else"."
~Lewis Carroll, *Alice's Adventures in Wonderland*

Dare

"IF I ADMIT right off that I was wrong, will that be enough to avoid a
whole conversation?"

I had just gotten back to the studio, two mammoth coffees in hand,
and that's the first thing Ingrid said as I walked in the door. I handed her
the cup with her standard order.

"I haven't seen you in three days and that's the first thing you say
to me?"

"Thanks, and good morning," she said, barely meeting my eye.

I had been prepared to tear her a new one, purposefully waiting
until she returned from her extended weekend away. She didn't come
back until now because she was afraid to face me—and I was letting her
get away with it because I knew she didn't mean to come off like an ass.

"I appreciate the apology, but we're still going to talk," I said, putting my coffee down on the desk I was leaning against. Meanwhile, she was staring down at her shoes.

"Jesus, 'grid, look at me."

She did.

"Just talk to me," I said. "What the hell were you thinking?"

She crossed her arms. "You *know* what I was thinking," she said. "I took one look at her and saw another pint-sized brunette staring up at you with those big eyes and I immediately thought, 'oh shit, here we go again.' And I realize it's been over a year, but I'm sorry Dare, I can't go through that again. I can't see *you* go through that again."

I ran my hand up and down my face, letting what she said sink in.

"They really are nothing alike."

She rolled her eyes. "I know that *now*," she said. "Chloe would've never stood up for herself the way Alice did last week. It was quite impressive, actually."

"Glad you think so," I scoffed.

"And not for nothing, but she's got a rack I'd want to dive into the deep end of and never come up for air."

I snorted-laughed. "Yeah, I bet."

She sighed. "I really am sorry."

"It's not me you need to be apologizing to."

She grimaced. "You can't just talk to her?"

"What are you, twelve? You've handled way worse," I said. "Besides, Alice is probably one of the most mature people I've ever known. She's not going to rake you over the coals."

"She wouldn't if she knew the whole story," Ingrid said, taking a sip of her coffee. "Have you had a chance to talk to her about what happened?"

I was avoiding and we both knew it.

"Right, that's what I thought," she said, shaking her head.

"I'll get to it," I said, staring off into nothing. "It's just . . . I wanted to have something that wasn't tainted, just for a little while longer. I mean, Jesus Christ, she's got to be the only person in New York City who doesn't know what happened. It's been like a gift, you know?"

She gave a sympathetic smile. "Yeah, of course. All the more reason why she needs to learn it from you, sooner versus later."

I blew out my exasperation.

"I'm debating on whether or not to include the work from that whole time, for my solo exhibit," I said. "What do you think?"

She shrugged. "You've never shown any of them to me, so it's kind of hard to give an opinion."

I had about a half dozen paintings and a bunch of photographs from my time with Chloe. "I haven't looked at any of it since then," I said.

"If you can't even look at them, probably not ready to show them."

I felt the muscle in my jaw tick.

"So, you'll apologize to Alice?"

"Yes, *fine*," she said. "The next time I see her."

I nodded, glancing at all the shit on her desk. I noticed a pile of invites for her group show, all addressed and stamped, ready to go. I fanned them out and spotted one with an Arkansas address.

She was sending one to her parents. That was a surprise. I sifted it out of the pile and eyed her.

She looked embarrassed.

"Look, I already know it's pathetic, my wanting them there. And I know they won't have the first clue what a big deal it is for me to have work showing at Sean Kelly Gallery, even if it is a group show. So go ahead and yell at me or—

I didn't even think. I stalked over and surrounded her in a big bear hug. "You don't have to explain one thing to me or anyone else, you hear?"

And just like that, she broke down and cried, something I think I may have seen her do maybe twice in the ten years I'd known her. I held her tight, feeling her rail thin frame wrench with sobs.

"I hate them," I said, my voice low and scary. "I've never even met them, but I absolutely despise them for what they've done to you."

"I know they suck, but I still love them, even after everything."

I kissed the top of her head, smoothing her hair down.

"Underneath all that hard shell there's a gooey center, isn't there?"

"Shut up," she said into my chest.

"A big softie," I went on.

"I am totally poisoning your lunch today."

Then she hugged me back, hard.

My chin was propped on the top of her electric blue head.

"You are talented and fierce," I whispered. "You've got an amazing work ethic, a big heart and you're rabidly loyal in a world full of sell-outs." I stopped and made sure she met my eye. "But if you're waiting for Barbara and Jim Peterson to validate you, you'll be lost for a long, long time. I'm not saying miracles can't happen, but I wouldn't keep a placeholder in my heart. You understand me?"

"I do," she said, catching her breath.

"They don't deserve you."

She shook her head. "It's not about what they deserve. It's about what I believe. And I will always, until the day I die, believe in love and redemption."

I stilled.

"Did you just sort of quote Wonder Woman to me?"

"Yeah, it was a really good movie, she said, wiping her tears and runny nose on my tee.

"That's okay. I didn't like this one anyway."

She cackled, and I felt the vibrations around my heart.

"You're my family, 'grid."

"You're all I have," she said in a small voice.

A vulnerable Ingrid, damn it, she's killing me.

"Hey," I said, holding her away from my body by her shoulders, so I could read her expression. "I'm not all you have, but maybe, you know, you might want to let some people in. Maybe, you know, graduate from the bar hook-ups, too?"

"Really? Uh, *okay*, Sean Penn."

She had a point. I wasn't exactly a people person. There was definitely no sunshine beaming out my ass.

"Alright, I'll let that go for now," I said.

"Appreciated."

"Oh, and before I forget, I don't want any more of those open studio parties on Thursdays. Not until you can figure out a better vetting system for the guest list. No more coked-up assholes like last month."

She took out her imaginary clipboard and pen. "Disinvite most people with money in Manhattan. Got it."

I frowned.

"So, when is the next time Alice is coming over to our little slice of Wonderland? I have an apology to deliver."

"She said she'll come by over the weekend," I said, finishing up the rest of my coffee and tossing the cup.

"Well, at least someone is changing patterns around here," she said.

My brows furrowed. "What do you mean?"

She snorted. "Chloe moved in after your first date. It's all or nothing with you." She must've seen something in my expression or body language because she cackled again. "Alice setting her boundaries must be driving you crazy."

Now, it was my turn. "Shut up, Ingrid."

But she was right. Not knowing when I was seeing Alice again was an itch under my skin I couldn't reach. I hated it and it was only Wednesday.

Fifteen

"What a strange world we live in . . ."
~Lewis Carroll, *Alice in Wonderland*

Alice

I HAD SAID goodbye to Dare early Tuesday morning.

I told him I wasn't going to come back until Friday.

But he was right. I missed him almost immediately.

Damn it. Why do I always catch feelings so fast?

Tuesday night, I laid in my twin-sized bed, trying to drown out the sound of my sister and some new guy. She may appear all prim and prude on the surface, but Caroline was a bona fide man-eater.

The only thing worse than growing up hearing your mother having sex in the next room is being all grown up and hearing your sister having sex in the next room. Now I know why she gifted me a pair of noise-cancelling headphones.

I almost caved by the next morning, especially when I got this text:

Dare: My sheets still smell of you, btw. I may never leave this bed.

Me: I like the way you smell, too. And I don't mean your cologne.

Dare: Whatever it takes. I'm not above using my olfactory arsenal to get you where I want.

I told him about our homework from my professor, about sharing sexual histories and fantasies. He told me he couldn't wait to hear all of mine.

That's when I panicked. Because I didn't have any—not really.

"I think I'm in the wrong field," I said to Lulu. We were out for drinks, just the two of us, at this bar called The Milky Way, which—who knew?—was *the* geek squad watering hole in Midtown. Lulu hardly ever drank, but it didn't seem to matter. From the second we walked in, it was evident she was their Queen and the nerd herd were her happy little drones.

"Why do you say that?" she asked, oblivious to all the men using their beer mugs as drool cups over her.

"Because my professor wants me to explore my 'hidden' fantasies and share them with Dare, and I've got nothing."

"Oh c'mon, that can't be true," she said, taking out her Coca Cola lip balm and rolling some onto her perfect, bee-stung lips. The guy next to her at the bar started choking on an olive just watching her.

"I know I have a dark side, but nothing specific appeals to me," I said, sloshing the ice around my glass.

"How about being tied up? Or spanked? Those are standard."

I shook my head. "I have too many control issues—and I did that with Chad back in the day and hated it."

I could see the wheels turning.

"Threesomes?"

"I don't share well," I said.

"Being the focus of a gang bang?"

"Seriously?" I asked.

She shrugged. "It's not my thing, but it's a fantasy for some."

"Next," I said.

"Okay . . . what about role playing?"

I looked around the bar. "Feels like a different thing when you say that in here, more like me in a golden bikini with a bunch of these Lesters pretending to be Jabba the Hut. No thanks."

She chuckled. "A fair point, but don't rule that out. It can be very hot."

The bartender came over with two more of our drinks.

"Hi ladies, these are compliments from the men at the end of the bar," he said, directing our gaze to the other end.

I was about to say 'thanks,' but Lulu interceded.

"Tell them it's appreciated, but we're here together," she said, her finger going back and forth between us. "I don't want to lead them on."

I could tell by the look on his face the bartender wasn't fully buying what Lulu was selling, but he said the right thing and went to deliver the bad news to the cast of *The Big Bang Theory* anyway.

"I wasn't interested in Howard or Raj either, but what was that about?" I asked.

She took the hair band off her wrist and threaded it through to make a ponytail. "If we had accepted, that would've given them the opening they wanted. And trust me, those two wouldn't be picking up on your 'don't enter my dance space' social cues."

"Whatever you say." I sipped my Jack.

"Okay, so not into dressing up or impact play," she said, strumming her fingers on the bar top. "No threesomes or group stuff either. Of course, there's breath play, age play, edge play, wax play . . ."

I downed the rest of my drink.

She stared. "Maybe you *are* in the wrong field."

I signaled for another. "Are you into any of those?"

She shrugged. "I've tried almost all of it, except for anything with bodily fluids. That's a hard limit."

"What are your go-to's, the ones you really like?"

Lulu swirled the straw in her virgin tropical drink. "I go through phases, just like anything else. It also depends upon the partner. Different people bring out different kinds of energies."

I nodded. "Before Dare, I've had three lovers my whole life."

Her eyes rounded. "You're kidding."

"Nope," I said before taking a healthy swig. "Two in high school, neither of those yahoos worth the ink used in my diary. And then, Chad."

"And now, Mr. Grangeworth," she smiled. "I like you and him together."

"I like him a lot. Too much," I said while tearing the bar napkin into strips.

"Why do you say that?"

"Because even though I'm out with you, I'm really sitting here thinking about him on a constant loop,"

She looked confused. "So?"

"That doesn't bother you? You don't feel insulted?"

Lulu shrugged. "That would be hypocritical. While you're thinking about Dare, I'm sitting here thinking about Beck. I can't even begin to express how disruptive it's become. I'm even having trouble focusing at work."

I smiled. "That's one of the many things I love about you, Lulu. You don't get bent out of shape over the little things."

I took a chance and placed my hand over hers. She usually wasn't comfortable with being touched, but she didn't flinch. "Thanks for hearing me out and being such an awesome friend. It means a lot, my Lulu Lemon."

She leaned in and gave me a hug.

Very un-Lulu-like.

"Oh wow. So, this is happening." I hugged her back. "What was that for?"

"Because this is the first time any of you have come to *me* for advice, It's usually the other way around," she said, blinking a lot, something she does when she's either really happy or nervous. "Thank you for trusting me, Alice."

"Excuse me, ladies?"

It was the bartender again. He had another round in his hands.

"Again?" I asked, exasperated.

"Yeah, but now *that* whole side of the bar wants to comp your drinks in exchange for getting the two of you kissing and permission to film it."

Sixteen

"You're entirely bonkers. But I'll tell you a secret: All the best people are."
~Lewis Carroll, *Alice in Wonderland*

Alice

I WASN'T DRUNK.

Okay, I wasn't *that* drunk.

Lulu had wanted to come with, but I told her no way, especially since Beck showed at the bar, looking for her. It was like the King of the Geeks coming to claim his Queen. They even got a round of applause.

That's when I knew I was done drinking for the night. Because I got the happy-weepies, telling Lulu how much I loved her and how happy I was for them. Then I informed Beck I loved him too because he had the good sense to be crazy about my girl.

I may be charming when tipsy, but I'm a blubbering sap when drunk.

Beck whisked Lulu away, but had his driver drop me off before they left.

So now, I was in front of Dare's building, totally thrilled to see him, but worried I was coming too soon, despite what he said. I pressed the studio buzzer, playing a 'shave and a haircut' beat. I waited for what felt like forever. I would've frozen to death, but I was all liquored up, so I felt nothing but a happy haze.

The door swung open.

It was Ingrid. *Ah, craptastic.*

"Bet you're thrilled to see me," I said, a little too loudly.

Her mouth twitched. "Well, *someone's* loaded."

"Loaded with charm and sass, thank you very much," I said, doing a half curtsey, followed by a pretend, kung-fu punch. "But don't mess with me. I'm from the South and we totally know how to throw down, down there."

She rolled her eyes. "Come on in, Bruce Lee," she said, holding the door open. I followed in, noticing most of the lights downstairs were off.

"You were shut down for the night, weren't you?" I asked, looking around, twirling in a circle. "I'm sorry I made you come down."

"I was up, anyway. Don't worry about it," she said, shuffling her feet. That's when I noticed she was wearing footie pajamas.

"Those look ultra-comfy."

"Yeah, they are, but listen. I've been wanting to talk to you."

I craned my head, looking for the flap.

And there it was. "Oh wow, it really *is* like the ones I used to wear as a kid," I said.

"Hard to believe you're getting a PhD in anything," Ingrid muttered, walking us to the elevator. "Can you please focus on what I'm trying to say to you?"

I met her eye. "What *are* you trying to say?"

She let out an exasperated breath. "That I'm sorry I gave you such a hard time the other day. It wasn't fair and it wasn't about you."

I stared at her for a few beats. "Appreciate the apology. That's mighty gracious of you."

The elevator dinged and opened. "After you, m'lady," I said.

That earned me some New York stink eye.

She hit one button for, where I assumed, she lived, and the top floor for me.

"He's already upstairs and knows you're coming," she said, legs out, weight leaning on the bar behind her.

Then it got quiet, which meant I had a moment to think.

"Whatever happened with Chloe must have been really messed up," I said.

Her gaze locked with mine. "Yeah, it really was."

I tried letting that sink in.

Sweet Jesus, what happened with that girl?

The elevator dinged again. We were at her floor.

"Night," I said.

"Goodnight, Alice," she said, stopping halfway out, her expression softening. "Make sure he tells you about her soon. And know, no matter what he says, it wasn't his fault and he is a really good guy. The best, actually."

I smiled. "Thanks, Ingrid."

The doors closed and the elevator whisked me up.

And that's when I started getting nervous, a million questions swirling through my Tennessee whisky-soaked brain.

Was this woman Chloe someone he still carried a torch for? Should I insist he tell me about her? How deep did I really want this thing between Dare and me to go? Sure, we're together and exclusive, but maybe we just keep it light.

Please, you're already falling hard and that man does not do casual.

And what about the whole reason why I got involved with him in the first place? This was supposed to be about my grad program. I had homework to do, damn it, and I couldn't think of one sexual fantasy.

How was that possible? What was *wrong* with me?

There were women entering convents who have more exciting sexual histories than I did.

Romance novels may wax poetic about alpha heroes loving them virginal heroines, but in real life, most men don't want to be saddled with a woman with such limited experience.

You could say my mind was spiraling. Just a bit.

The elevator dinged and the doors opened.

He was waiting for me, hair damp, only wearing a towel.

Sweet baby Jesus, is he my prize for being good?

His gorgeous face split with his smile, but I held my hand out, standing between the elevator doors.

"I've got something to say and I need to get it all out before you mush my brain with your hot-guy mojo," I said, waving my hand up and down to illustrate my point.

He let that sink in for a total of two seconds before he busted out laughing, grabbing my hand and pulling me into his arms.

"Hey!"

He beamed down at me.

"How much did you have to drink?" he asked.

Dare's arms were wrapped around me real tight, but I managed to wiggle my hand free to hold up three fingers.

"Well, that's not much at all," he said.

"I'm known in many parts of Carolina as a lightweight."

That earned another ear-to-ear grin. "So, what did you want to tell me?"

I made a raspberry sound. "Well, now my brain's full of cotton, 'cuz I'm surrounded by all that mojo of yours I was talking about."

His left brow quirked up. "You know, your Southern accent gets a lot stronger when you've had a few."

"I do know. I know all 'bout it."

He bent down, the tip of his nose and his lips brushing along my neck.

"Damn it, Dare, you know that move makes me shiver."

"All I know is I've been missing you. If you hadn't shown up here, I would've been at your place," he whispered as his lips, tongue, and teeth teased my ear. I felt a rush of wet between my legs and my nipples got hard.

I let out a whimper.

"Fuck, Dixie, you can't make sounds like and expect me to hold off."

He pressed his length between my legs, rocking into me as he grabbed my ass with both hands. My body was on fire.

I didn't think. Both my legs wrapped around his waist just as his towel dropped and the elevator dinged, still open.

Remember, share your sexual fantasies with your partner.

Get out of your comfort zone.

"Fuck me in the elevator, Dare."

"It's not private," he warned.

I pushed my cleft into him. "I don't care."

He didn't need to be told twice. He went right in, slamming us against the inside wall. The doors closed.

"Shit, I don't have a condom," he said, panting into my hair. "But I swear, I'm clean."

"Me too," I said. "I trust you."

"Fuck, I need in there," he said as his mouth crashed over mine. I shoved my hands in his hair, fisted it hard. And I knew he got off on it when he groaned down my throat. One of his hands left my ass long enough to push my panties to the side, take his cock and align it with my opening.

"I can't go slow or gentle," he said. "Tell me now."

I could barely see straight, I wanted him so much.

"Fuck me, City. And do it like you mean it."

"Fuck!" he screamed as his cock slammed home.

"OhMyGosh," I cried out.

I have never felt so stretched and full.

He told no lies because Dare Grangeworth, buck naked in an elevator, rammed that gorgeous dick deep and hard inside, moving his hips in such a way that he was hitting all the right angles.

Then the doors shut and the car started going down. Neither of us slowed.

Instead, he pressed his weight into my body, so he could reach my cleft with his calloused fingers, making magic radiate all over.

The elevator car stopped but I was right at the edge of the cliff.

"I'm so close, baby," I said. "I need just a lil' bit of pressure."

"You got it," he groaned, giving my clit the perfect pinch and flicker.

And that did it. My back arched off the elevator wall as I came hard all over his length. A white, hot flash burned my eyes behind my lids as my body convulsed in pleasure.

"Shit, you're so tight," he moaned into my neck, seconds before his grunt turned into a roar, his orgasm making his body shudder all around me.

Another flash went off, but this time I opened my eyes.

The elevator was opened and there were two guys standing there, watching us.

One of them spoke. "Hey, aren't you Dare Grangeworth?"

"What the fuck, man?" he yelled as he held onto me while hitting the button on the console. The doors shut and the car moved up.

I couldn't help it. I started cracking up.

"Two strange guys got to see us fucking. How are you laughing about this?" he asked.

"Because on my way over here, I was freaking out that I didn't have some hot fantasy to share and maybe I was in the wrong field."

"Seriously?"

The look on his face was priceless and I bit my lip to try to stop laughing.

"Uh yeah, but I'm thinking I was thinking too much," I added. "Note for your files, I do that—a lot."

That made us both crack up.

His gaze found mine, going all soft and lazy on me. It was beautiful.

"I'm glad you're all good, but every time you laugh, your pussy strangles my dick."

So much for sappy.

"Oh, hush up," I said as I gave a playful slap on his shoulder as he eased me down. "There are worse ways to suffer."

We got back inside and cleaned up. I wore his robe, which was a cotton weave that molded like a second skin to my body. All he had on was pajama pants, hung low on his hips, giving me full view of his magnificent, muscled torso. A woman could spend days exploring the planes and ridges of a body like that and never get enough.

"Babe, if you keep looking at me like that, there's going to be consequences," he said as he laid back on the couch, legs open.

This sounds interesting. "What kind of consequences?"

He grinned. "The kind leading to you coming hard and me getting to watch."

I felt those words right between my legs.

He patted his thigh. "Come here already."

"But my hair's still damp."

He gave a look.

I pretended to be exasperated. "Okay, *fine*," I said, crawling over and lying on him, my back to his front.

He started flipping through the movie channels. "What are you in the mood to watch?" he asked.

"Something light," I said. "If you can stand it, maybe a rom-com?"

I looked up to find him with a huge smile on his face.

"What?" I asked.

"Nothing, baby," he said, giving me a squeeze. "As you wish."

I let out a soft laugh. "A gorgeous, talented manly man who quotes *Princess Bride* and doesn't mind watching sappy rom-coms with his woman? Who *are* you, Dare Grangeworth?"

"That's simple. I'm yours," he said, kissing the top of my head.

He stopped flipping through the channels. "This one's a classic. Ever seen *The Goodbye Girl?*"

"I haven't."

"Well then, Dixie, you're in for a treat."

Seventeen

"The White Rabbit put on his spectacles.
'Where shall I begin, please your Majesty?' he asked.
'Begin at the beginning,' the King said gravely,
'and go on till you come to the end: then stop.'"
~Lewis Carroll, *Alice's Adventures in Wonderland*

Dare

"IF I LIVE through this, remind me to never, under any circumstances, do this again. Got it?"

Ingrid's head jerked. "Are you sniffing glue? You're going to be hanging in the Guggenheim, while you're still alive. And it's a solo show. Artists are lotto-lucky if they score even one of these and you're already bitching about not doing another one?"

Leave it to Ingrid to always give me perspective.

"Where's Alice?" she asked.

"She's at school for the day," I told her, thumbing through some of my old photographs. "But she'll be back tonight and will stay through the weekend."

"Good. I like her," she said. "Don't fuck it up."

"Nice," I said, listening but not listening. Something was gnawing at me.

"What?" she asked, arms crossed.

I eyed her before looking back at the work I had already done.

No way was this good enough.

"You and I know the only reason why I got the Guggenheim show . . ." I trailed off. I couldn't even say it out loud.

"Finish what you were going to say," she said, searching my face.

"It's certainly not because I'm at that level of talent," I said.

She frowned. "That's bullshit," she said, then something behind her eyes shifted. "You think the only reason you got the show is because of Chloe's death."

"Well, of course I think that. Because it's true."

"It's *not* true," she insisted. "You've sold out every show you've had since coming back to New York. Your mixed-medium work has been heralded as the bridge between photorealism and postmodern art. No one does what you do."

I gave a quick nod. She came over to where I was standing, feet wide and arms crossed in front of me. Her small hand rested on my forearm.

"What happened with Chloe does not define you as an artist," she said.

"I know that."

Ingrid peered at me. "Do you?"

Just then, someone hit the front door buzzer.

"I'll get it," Ingrid said, taking the stairs because it was faster.

It wasn't too long before I heard her voice over the studio intercom.

"Um, Dare? You need to come down. Right away."

She sounded worried. And now I was worried because nothing rattled Ingrid.

I slid down the stair rails and barreled through the double doors, leading to the main studio floor. She was at her desk, with a newspaper opened on top.

"What is it?" I asked, coming up next to her.

"A friend of mine saw this and dropped it off just now," she said, turning the pages to the front.

It was this morning's edition of the *New York Daily Post*.

And there was a picture of my bare ass, dick deep in Alice, in the

elevator last night. The headline read "Art World's Bad Boy on a Wild Ride with Mystery Woman."

"Shit," I said, pulling at the end of my beard. "When I find those two dipshits, I'm going to shove their camera phones so far up their asses . . ."

"At least you have a nice ass," she said, chuckling to herself.

I gave her a look.

"What? Hey, just because I'm not looking to tap that, doesn't mean I can't appreciate its aesthetic value."

I grimaced, scanning the article.

"I'll save you the trouble," she said. "The article mentions Chloe, saying how 'the people of New York' wondered if you were going to ever move on."

"Thank Christ Alice was still dressed," I said.

"Speak for yourself, I was hoping for a peek at those luscious breasts of hers."

I blew out a frustrated breath while folding the newspaper and tucking it under my arm. "My girl is not into attention, especially this kind."

She shrugged. "Text her. Better coming from you first, right?"

I looked at the time. She would be in class until late afternoon.

"I have so much to do for the show," I said more to myself than to Ingrid.

"Listen, you go and I'll sort through all your work. You have a lot here, Dare, more than you realize. The show's supposed to be a mid-career retrospective, right?"

"Yeah."

"Okay then," she said as she started to move pieces to different areas of the room. "By the time you get back, you can decide what goes in the show."

"That'll work . . . I owe you, Ingrid," I said.

Something passed over her. "Dare, you found me ankle deep in a dumpster, weighing eighty-five pounds, looking for any scraps of food and art supplies I could find. It took three treatments to get all the lice out of my hair and too many doctor visits to count, to heal the rest of my body. You never once made a pass at me or made me feel I owed you for anything you gave.

"But more than that, in a world that was more than willing to throw me out, like *I* was garbage, you loved me unconditionally, giving me living proof there is a God, that He loves me and is looking out for me. If I lived a thousand lifetimes, you wouldn't owe me a damn thing, Dare DeMarco Grangeworth.

"Now, get out of here so I can work-and find your woman and make everything okay for her like you did with me."

Eighteen

"If everybody minded their own business,
the world would go around a great deal faster than it does."
~Lewis Carroll, *Alice in Wonderland*

Alice

"WHO'S GOING TO tell her?"

"Her advisor should do it, not another student."

"If it were me, I would die of embarrassment."

"Why? She's done nothing wrong. She's expressing her sexuality without worrying about the male gaze."

"True, but who's going to take her seriously in academia after *that*?"

Those were just some of the whisperings I heard as I was walking in between classes. Frankly, I was dying to ask who they were talking about, but I didn't know any of them well enough. Besides, as soon as they saw me, they shut their traps and dispersed like waterbugs getting caught with the lights on.

If I was the paranoid type, I'd be worried.

"Not my circus, not my monkeys," I muttered under my breath, on my way to my last lecture of the day-a three-hour seminar on gender and sexuality.

But what I was really thinking about was my elevator 'ride'. I know that, for

many, doing it in an elevator was no big thing, but for me it was. A younger me would have thought my more experimental, bolder approach was because of Dare. It certainly helped to have an open partner, instead of someone, like Chad, who had the same three moves and felt threatened at the mere suggestion of anything else.

But that elevator ride was my idea, a fantasy I didn't even know I had until the opportunity presented itself. Maybe someday, I'd want hot wax poured all over my breasts or feel a need to dress up like baby doll and beg daddy to spank me. Didn't feel like either would ever be my thing, but who knows?

Man plans and God laughs.

What I did know was that I'd been so afraid of my own sexuality that I had never given myself permission to let my body and mind dream in its own language. How could they? I'd been too busy looking over my shoulder, trying to rise above the whisperings about my mama. When someone you love has a bad reputation, especially in a small town, everyone thinks that's your story, too. I couldn't begin to count how many guys thought they were entitled to a piece of me, how many I had to fight off.

They may not have had me in the biblical sense, but that doesn't mean they didn't get their pound of flesh by stealing a piece of my soul.

Well, as of now, I was taking them all back.

Rihanna sang in my head: *baby, this is what you came for.*

So true, Ri-Ri, so true.

I was just about to walk into my seminar when my advisor's assistant, Jennifer, snagged my arm. She was usually bouncy and all smiles, like a new puppy, but not today.

"What's wrong? You look like you just found out Chevy stopped making trucks or something."

She didn't laugh, and Jen always laughed at my Southern funnies.

"Alice, the professor needs to speak with you, right away," she said, wringing her hands.

"But I have a class 'bout now," I said, pointing my thumb towards the faculty lounge where my seminar met. "Can't it wait?"

She shook her head. "I'm afraid not. She wants to see you right away," she said, eyeing the people in the lounge. "I'll have a word with Professor Tisdale and let her know why you're missing today."

I stared, dumbfounded.

"Go on. She's waiting for you in her office."

I nodded and started walking, trying to imagine what could possibly have happened. I took my phone out of my pocket, turning it back on, so I could call my sister. I needed to make sure she was okay, because that's the only reason I could imagine I'd be summoned like this.

As soon as I got a signal, I saw a bunch of texts from Dare, telling me he was on his way to campus and that he needed to talk right away.

Okay, now I thought I might throw up. If anything happened to her . . . no, I couldn't even conceive of a world without my sister. She was my family, my best friend, my mentor, and frankly, a second mama.

I ignored his texts and called Caroline. She picked up on the second ring.

"What's up, buttercup?" she said, all cheery and bright.

I couldn't breathe. I leaned my weight against one of the building, crouching down, trying to calm myself.

"Alice? Alice!" She was freaking out now. "Talk to me, honey. What's wrong?"

I was still panting. "I'm fine," I eked out. "I thought . . . something had happened to you."

"To me? No, sister. I'm right as rain. Why would you think such a thing?"

I coughed into my hand. "Because I've been summoned to my advisor's office and Dare's been texting, saying he needs to talk to me right away . . . I thought they were prepping me for bad news."

I heard her breathe a sigh of relief. "I'm sure one has nothing to do with the other."

"Yeah, you're right," I said, feeling better already. "Had to check though."

"Aren't you the one always telling me that professors are the most obtuse, entitled creatures on the planet?" She didn't wait for my answer. "I betcha she's just impatient and thinks you should stop everything when she calls. She probably needs some help and expects you on it, right quick."

"Yeah, okay. I better get over there then. I'll talk to you later."

We said our goodbyes and I headed to my advisor's office.

I barely had to knock before she called me in.

My advisor was one of those professors who insisted you call her by her first name. Of course, being a Southerner, using the Christian name of an authority figure felt as wrong as wearing a mini skirt to church.

"Hi Alice, come in, come in," she said, gesturing towards the chair in front of her desk. "Thank you for coming so quickly. Oh, and would you shut the door?"

"Sure, Ms. Joan," I said, doing what she asked and taking a seat.

She smiled. "You're the only student I've ever had who called me 'Ms.' Joan."

I shrugged. "If I didn't show some kind of deference, the ghosts of all my ancestors would roll over in their graves, but not before they popped in and slap me on the side of my head, for showing such disrespect," I teased.

She gave a half-hearted laugh.

Okay, I'm guessing the idle chit-chat portion of our scheduled program is done. Now onto business.

"I've called you in today, to discuss a delicate matter," she said, leaning back in her leather chair. "And it's delicate because, well frankly, we've never had to address a matter like this before, at least not with a student."

I was utterly confused, but I was hoping to catch her gist soon.

"There is some precedence," she continued. "We have one professor who made a series of pornographic films back in the seventies under a pseudonym. We have another who writes erotica, again under a pseudonym. But your case is quite different."

"I'm sorry, but I have no idea what you're talking about."

Her mouth gaped, but she recovered fast enough. She adjusted her glasses on the bridge of her nose. "Well then . . ." She opened one of her drawers and took out a folded newspaper. She handed it to me.

I felt my forehead wrinkle.

"Go on," she said. "Read it."

I unfolded the paper, only to find myself on the cover.

With Dare and his bare ass.

In the elevator.

Fucking.

With my 'O' face, mouth wide, mid-orgasm.

The headline read: Art World's Bad Boy on a Wild Ride with Mystery Woman.

My ears started ringing.

My hands started to shake.

"I-I-I . . . how did this happen?" I asked, but not really asking.

Then, I remembered, the flash of white I felt behind my eyelids.

I thought it had been my body's release, but it was the camera flash, from those two guys waiting for the elevator.

I glanced up to find her looking quite uncomfortable.

Oh shit. Please don't let this be for the reason I think it is.

"Are you kicking me out of school?"

She grimaced. "There will be a hearing in two weeks. A decision will be made then."

My stomach lurched and tears welled in my eyes.

"This was printed without my knowledge nor my consent," I said.

She gave a sweet smile. "I assumed. That will count for something."

Ms. Joan walked over to the mini fridge she kept in her office, taking out a bottle of water and handing it to me.

"Thanks," I scratched out.

She placed her hand on my shoulder. "Jennifer will email you all the information about the hearing. You are allowed one faculty member to speak on your behalf. I would be honored if you chose me."

I grabbed a tissue off her desk and nodded. "Yes, thank you. Of course."

I blew my nose.

"I'll give you some privacy."

She walked out of her office and closed the door behind her.

And that's when I let out the real, ugly cry.

My whole body shook. I went through one tissue, then three, then five.

Everything I had worked for was going to wash away.

I tried to stop crying, but the sobs kept coming, as if this bad news had uncorked some secret well of tears I had inside. I was drowning in self-pity.

If you hadn't been with someone famous, you would've never ended up on the cover of some rag.

I knew it wasn't Dare's fault. My guess was that he was livid and trying to get to me to make sure I was okay. But I wasn't okay. Not even close.

Below the picture, there was an article, but since they had no idea who I was, they used their column inches to discuss Chloe and the foot-steps I was walking in.

His former dancer-turned-photographer girlfriend of three years, the daughter of a prominent New York family. There were rumors she suffered from a variety of mental health issues. Dare was commended for standing by her, even after two psychiatric stays.

In fact, everyone thought she had been through the worst of it. She seemed happy, making plans to teach dance to little girls in a studio on the Upper East Side.

So, imagine their surprise when one day she went to the top of her parents' building and jumped out the window.

No warning.

No note.

They couldn't even use dental records to identify her, the damage was so bad.

She was twenty-four years old.

The family went on a crusade, blaming him for her instability, saying she had been a happy person until they got together. But her former classmates and teachers and other relatives were quoted saying that Chloe had always been emotionally fragile.

Dare hadn't been seen in the press until the photo of us came to light. *Bet those morons got a good price for it, too.*

They ran two small photos under the fold line, one of Chloe by herself and another with the two of them, walking arm-in-arm, in Central Park.

She had long, brown hair and big eyes, with one of those tiny, dancer bodies. She was beautiful, but delicate, like you could break her in half. In the photo, she was looking up at him, as if he was her whole world.

I'd seen enough. I folded the paper back up and stuck it in my bag, and left a note for Ms. Joan.

I took out a compact and cleaned myself up as best I could. My eyes were bloodshot and the tip of my nose was bright red. I was a mess, but I didn't really care.

I left the office and walked across campus to hop on the subway. Thank goodness, I didn't bump into anyone. Then, I recalled all the gossip I heard earlier that morning.

"Who's going to tell her?"

"Her advisor should do it, not another student."

"If it were me, I would die of embarrassment."

"Why? She's done nothing wrong. She's expressing her sexuality without worrying about the male gaze."

"True, but who's going to take her seriously in academia after that?"

They were talking about me the whole time and I was too dumb to know it.

I am a rube, a moron, a country-bumpkin simpleton.

Dear Lord, I was over five hundred miles away from home and I was still being called a whore. Only this time, I couldn't blame my mama. This was all on me.

"Alice?" I heard behind me.

I knew that voice. Just this morning, that voice both stirred and soothed me.

I turned around.

Still as beautiful, probably even more famous.

"Jesus, Dixie, are you okay?"

There will be a hearing next week.

I may be kicked out of school.

"No, Dare, I'm not okay. I don't know if anything's going to be okay again."

Nineteen

"It either brings tears to their eyes, or else . . ."
"Or else what?" said Alice,
for the Knight had made a sudden pause.
"Or else it doesn't, you know."
~Lewis Carroll, *Alice in Wonderland*

Dare

I SHOULDN'T HAVE waited so long to tell her about Chloe. All I wanted was a little more time in the bubble. I should've also made precautions to protect our privacy, but I let myself get caught up in the moment. Man, that was really stupid.

Her hand was still out, like a human stop sign, so I raised both of mine in surrender. "I get it. You're pissed and embarrassed, but I swear on my life, I had nothing to do with that photo and, as soon as I find out who those punks are, I'm going to take care of everything."

Her eyes were glassy and red-rimmed. She shook her head, arms folded in front of her like a shield. "I never thought for one second you were behind that photo, Dare, and the damage is already done."

I wanted to hold her in the worst way.

"I know you're a private person. I should have been more careful, to protect you."

A cold wind blew, making her teeth rattle. She had on a thin jacket, the kind that probably kept someone warm in North Carolina, but wouldn't cut it here. I took off my jacket as I went to her, putting it around her shoulders.

"That's very gentlemanly of you. Thank you," she said.

"Anytime," I said. *I'd give you anything. All you have to do is ask.*

Her shivering stopped and she gave a small smile. "I'm sorry about what happened to Chloe. I read about it in the paper."

I sucked in the cold air. "I should have told you about it sooner."

"I don't blame you for not wanting to relive it, why you delayed talking about it."

Damn it, she really is perfect for me.

"I loved her. I was crazy about her," I said, my hands in my pockets as I stared off. "In the beginning, I got off on her needing me so much. I thought of myself as her protector. Man, I was so stupid and full of myself . . ."

"Dare, you couldn't have known," she said, taking a small step towards me.

I shook my head. "No, I couldn't have. God knows her parents were in deep denial. But when I came home late from a show and I found her surrounded by shards of glass, her cutting herself . . . I insisted she be hospitalized. She went and got better. She went on meds. But then, she'd either go off them or they'd stop working."

"What did she have?" she asked.

"Bipolar II, Borderline Personality Disorder . . . those were the major hitters."

She didn't know what to say. No one ever did.

"I hated how she died," I said, looking at the ground, "But I'd be lying if I didn't admit I was relieved to not have to ride that rollercoaster anymore. And I feel like a piece of shit for admitting that out loud, but that's the truth.

"I know it's not on me how she died, but I still blame myself for letting my ego think I could've fixed her in the first place."

She stared at me, something working behind her eyes.

"I thought I could give Chad a soul," she said, shaking her head. "He showed me his softer side, something not really allowed in his household. It was survival of the fittest over there. I thought I could save him from all that. Turned out he didn't want to be saved after all."

Something passed between us.

Alice understood. She got me in a way no one did.

And that's when I realized, I loved this woman. It hadn't been long, but I didn't give a fuck.

I didn't feel a lick of the cold. My blood was racing too fast through my veins. I felt like I was on fire.

"I may get kicked out of school," she said, her voice soft and defeated.

The fire inside turned to ice. "You're shitting me."

She shook her head, examining her boots. Anything, probably, not to look at me.

"I was feeling so good this morning, too," she went on. "Like I was *finally* finding my way, being an integrated, sexual being."

I grasped the front of my jacket around her, pulling her close. "Don't let one photo take that away from you."

But it was like she didn't hear me.

"No matter what I do, I'm always going to be walking around with a scarlett letter on my chest," she said. "I don't know what I'll do if they kick me out."

"I'll hire an attorney," I said, hoping like hell she'd get that she was not alone in this. "Let me help you, Dixie."

She looked up, finally meeting my eyes. She appeared so lost and angry at the same time. Alice shrugged off my jacket and handed it off, like it was something dirty.

"Thanks for the offer," she said, looking uncomfortable. "I know you mean well, but this is why I didn't want to get involved in the first place."

My head reared back, like I had been slapped.

I just got her and I'm already losing her.

"So, what are you saying? You regret being with me?" I asked.

"No, it's just, I can't afford anything to distract me from what I came here to do," she said, letting out a sigh. "If you weren't so well known, maybe things could be different, but I can't spend my life looking over my shoulder, paranoid that every move we make may end up in a gossip rag."

I grimaced. "Well, I can't promise nothing like that will happen in the future. Shit happens, Alice. If you start walling yourself off from life, at twenty-five, your world's going to get narrow real fast."

She hoisted her backpack onto her shoulder. "I'm sorry. I just can't is all . . . bye, City."

Then, she got as far away from me as possible. I watched her walk away, getting smaller and smaller.

It was almost dark and the temperature had dropped. I put my jacket back on and cursed under my breath because it already smelled like her.

I started walking home, even as the ground crumbled beneath my feet. As what she said sunk in, my limbs and lungs turned to ice and ash.

She had brought me back to life. And I returned the favor by killing her career before it started.

Maybe Chloe's parents had been right all along. I was nothing but misery and pain.

Twenty

"It sounded an excellent plan, no doubt,
and very simply and neatly arranged; the only difficulty was,
that she had not the smallest idea how to set about it."
~Lewis Carroll, *Alice in Wonderland*

Alice

"YOU'VE BEEN HERE less than two months and already you made Page Six. Girl, that's hella impressive."

"Right Rayna, because that's every little girl's dream. I'll make sure my sister adds it to her CV of accomplishments."

Yeah, you could say my sister was madder than a wet cat.

I had texted all my girls on the way home, calling for an emergency tea party, which was code for when one of us had been knocked into next week by something bad happening.

"Please, it's not like she made a porno," Rayna bit back. "She's not even nude in the shot. Trust me, the hearing is just a formality."

Lulu hunched her shoulders. "I don't know. Academia is notoriously rigid and insular, even if Alice *is* studying human sexuality."

The others gave her death stares.

"Or, uh . . . maybe that's just how it was in my department," Lulu backtracked. "I'm sorry. I really am trying to help."

"You're fine, Lulu," I said, holding out my glass. "That wine should just say 'drink me bitches' because that what I'm doing all night."

Rayna poured my glass to the brim.

Caroline eyed me.

"What?" I said, feeling like I was shrinking right in front of everyone.

"I just think you should be preparing for your hearing, instead of drinking with us and making yourself feel better," my sister said.

"Wow, that's harsh," Lulu muttered.

Rayna's eyes rounded. "*Joder,* your sister doesn't play."

"What the hell, Ro?" I said, using a very old nickname for her.

Her expression softened, her hand covering mine. "You've just worked so hard. I don't want anything to get in your way."

I patted her hand. "You've got nothing to worry about," I said, taking a healthy sip. "I'm meeting with my advisor tomorrow to go over my statement. And I kind of broke it off with Dare."

My sister's face paled. "You did what?"

"Why would you do that?" Lulu asked.

"Did he give you a hard time? Blame *you* for the photo?" Rayna asked, looking ready to shiv something in the neck.

"No, of course not," I reassured them. "He found me on campus today, just to make sure I was okay." Now that I thought about it, that was mighty sweet of him.

"So, you're punishing him, for something out of his control?" Caroline asked, her lips pressing into a thin line.

I put my wine glass down. "The whole point of coming to New York was to make a life *I* created. Here, I'm not the daughter of the town trollop or the country bumpkin girlfriend of Carolina's favorite son. I'm just Alice, someone who rises and falls based on my actions, on my own merits. I'm not here the equivalent of a New York minute and I'm already going to be labeled Dare Grangeworth's Page Six girl. I may get kicked out of school over this. Sorry, but I don't need this kind of hassle."

They all just stared at me, giving each other knowing eyes in between.

"Listen, please just help me get through the hearing, okay? I can't think about anything until then, least of all, Dare Grangeworth."

Caroline put her hand out. "We've got your back, sister."

Rayna joined her hand with Caroline's. "Absolutely. That committee won't know what hit them."

"Worse comes to worse, I can build you a bomb or the perfect computer virus to infect their server," Lulu added.

I had started putting my hand in, but stopped. "Uh, maybe you can hold off on utilizing the weapons of mass destruction in your personal arsenal?"

Caroline muttered. "She really *is* a hairsbreadth away from becoming a supervillain, isn't she?"

Lulu rolled her eyes. "No fun. No fun at all."

"Did you just sass me, Lulu Lemon?"

"I believe I did," she said, a self-satisfied smile peeking through.

I put my hand in with the others. "If Lulu can deliver sass and sarcasm, then anything is possible. Let's *do* this thing."

Twenty-One

Alice: "How long is forever?"
White Rabbit: "Sometimes just one second."
~Lewis Carroll, *Alice in Wonderland*

Dare

"STOP DOING THAT," I told her, slapping her hand out of her mouth.

She was biting her nails.

"I can't help it," she said. "I do this when I'm nervous."

"If you don't cut it out, I'm going to hold your arms down. You know what that means."

Ingrid's whole face contorted. It wasn't that she thought I smelled, per se, but she wasn't a fan of anything masculine. She said that even when men were freshly showered, she could still smell what she called our 'man-stink' which was a combination of testosterone and cortisol.

I should mention that to Alice. She'd get a kick out of it.

Then I remembered, she broke up with me. We were done.

Alice wasn't mine anymore.

Yeah, I was feeling a little sorry for myself.

Then I felt a slap on the side of my head.

"Jesus 'grid! What's your problem?"

"Snap out of it," Ingrid said. "I know you miss her. And I miss you being . . . happy."

I rubbed my head for a couple of seconds, but took the hint.

"This is *your* night," I told her. "And you're right. I am here for you," I took her hand in mine. "So, you're going to have to deal with my man-stink for a little while because: one, I need to prevent you from eating your whole hand and, two, I want you to lead me through this crowd and show me where your work is before I get lost."

We were at her group show, *Thirty Artists Under Thirty*, and the place was packed. I had taken Ingrid out shopping for a new outfit and made her get a haircut. The results were stunning. Her electric blue hair was in a smart pixie cut and she wore a metallic red jumpsuit with matching red lipstick.

The press was going crazy for her look and her work. I felt like a proud papa.

Eventually, I noticed her nerves had calmed, and I let go of her hand and stepped back, so she could do her thing all on her own. Once I did, I saw all three of her paintings had been sold, each with their own little red dot.

I couldn't keep the smile off my face.

She did it. She's on her way.

I took a few photos of her as she was talking with the art critic of *The New York Times*. They were chatting like old friends.

"It wasn't that long ago you were standing there, just like she is now."

I knew that voice.

I turned around.

"Wow, I didn't expect to see you here," I said, taking her in.

"That's the kind of greeting I get?" she balked. "What's the phrase your mother taught me? 'Come in for the real thing.'"

I bent down and gave her a tight hug. It had been too long.

She broke away, but held both my hands in hers, giving them a squeeze.

"Where is your mother, by the way?" she asked.

"She's in Italy, taking cooking lessons and drinking wine without her son telling her to take it easy."

She smiled. "Well, good for her. She deserves it. But I have to say . . . you look like complete and utter shit."

I busted out laughing. "Thanks, Mrs. Grangeworth. Way to kick a man when he's down."

She threw her hands up, followed by a little shimmy. "It's the one advantage to being old. I can say and do whatever I want."

"Please, you've been this way for years. It's not age, it's moxie."

She winked while shooting a finger gun at me. "Right you are," she said.

A flash blinded my eyes. The press had descended and were taking photos.

Then came the questions.

"Are you here with your elevator hook-up?"

"Is it over?"

"Who is she anyway?"

I was ready to lose it, but Mrs. Grangeworth patted my lapel with her hand.

"I've got this," she muttered under her breath.

"My stepson Dare, was kind enough to be my companion for this epic art event. I am sure he will reveal the identity and status of his relationship with the young lady when the time is right. But for now, don't spoil an old woman's fun. Back off and bother Iris Apfel over there. She actually thinks she's Tweetie Bird in that yellow feather disaster."

They scattered, just like that.

"You haven't lost your touch," I said.

"You better believe it," she said, her gaze scanning my face. "Walk me outside. My driver should be arriving any minute."

I offered her my arm, which she took.

"Did I ever tell you how I met your father?"

That was out of left field, but fine, I'd bite.

"Nope, I missed that bedtime story."

She let out a throaty laugh. "Don't be cute. My heart can't take it," she said. "Anyway, he was vacationing with his family in Cape Cod, where I was working for the summer. He said he knew right away he was going to marry me. I worked at a hot dog stand, by the way. He must have bought over fifty of those awful things before I agreed to go out with him."

"So you knew then?" I asked, making sure she wasn't getting crushed by the crowd.

"All I knew was that I found him intriguing and that he scared the heck out of me. He was a Grangeworth. You know what my maiden name was? Polinski. Doesn't exactly scream money or connections."

"I didn't know that," I said.

We were finally outside, but her driver hadn't arrived yet.

The check girl ran out, with her fur. "Mrs. Grangeworth! You forgot your coat!"

I took it from her and gave a tip. I helped her put it on.

"Thank you, darling," she said, beaming up at me. "I wonder who taught you to always have a few extra dollars in your pocket?"

I chuckled. "You did," I said, smiling down at her.

She nodded. "You know, I loved my husband very much. And he loved me and he loved your mother. The heart wants what the heart wants."

You're an incredible lady. He didn't deserve you.

She wasn't done. "He loved me so much, he thought it would hurt me to know about you, because I couldn't have children . . . what a schmuck."

"Excuse me?"

"He would've gotten such a kick out of you," she sighed, shaking her head. "Men can be short-sighted. But so can young girls who feel out of their depths, especially in a new city."

I met her penetrating gaze.

She leaned closer. "Don't give up on her. She's scared out of her mind. Alice has had to work for every scrap she's gotten and she's afraid one mistake will make it all go away."

I stilled. "Wait a second, how do you know her name? How do you know anything about her?"

The driver pulled up, rushing to open her door.

She patted my cheek. "Because I look after those I love, but don't tell anybody. I have a reputation as a raging piece of work to uphold." She winked and got into her car. "And bring her by. I'll pretend she's my daughter and show her off at the club. I love it when I make Kathy Hilton feel so bad she eats her feelings."

Twenty-Two

"Lastly, she pictured to herself how this same little
sister of hers would, in the after-time, be herself a grown
woman; and how she would keep, through all her riper years,
the simple and loving heart of her childhood: and how she
would gather about her other little children, and make their
eyes bright and eager with many a strange tale, perhaps
even with the dream of Wonderland of long ago."
~Lewis Carroll, *Alice in Wonderland*

Alice

"CAN I READ your statement?"

It was the night before my hearing and I must have written and re-written the damn thing a hundred times. I was so fried I was apologizing in my sleep. I tossed the legal pad to my sister, rubbing my eyes with the heels of my palms.

"Sure, take a look. I've got like, a dozen different versions there."

She gave a tight smile, picked up the pad and sat down in her favorite chair. Caroline had just gotten home from work and looked wiped, but I

THE WONDER OF YOU   157

knew she was pushing all that aside to help me any way she could.

It was a special kind of hell, watching someone read what you wrote.

"Can I get you something to drink?" I asked.

She shook her head, her eyes not leaving the page.

I sat back and waited. I was not a patient person by nature.

It seemed to take her forever. I wanted to close my eyes in the worst way, but then I might fall asleep and I knew that would really peeve her off.

"Okay, I'm done," she said, keeping the pad in her lap.

"And?"

She met my eye. "You know I love you."

"Of course," I said without hesitation. "Wow, that must have really sucked if you're starting with the 'I love you' speech. Didn't you like *any* of the drafts?"

"No," she said.

"Great," I mumbled.

She smiled. "Do you know how over-the-moon proud I am of you?"

My throat got all tight. "Ro, don't you start now."

I could tell by her expression, she wasn't playing.

"It's always been you and me. No matter what deadbeats mom brought home. No matter what all the busybodies said in town, it's always been you and me, the Leighton sisters."

She got up from her chair and sat right on the edge of the coffee table, elbows pressed to her knees, her upper body leaned forward. She took my hands in hers.

"I thought I had done right by you," she said.

My eyes almost popped out of my head. "You did. You have!"

She shushed me. "I taught you how to put on make-up. I remember teaching you how to use a tampon when you got your period. I was the one who took you to buy your first bra down at the Walmart. I also taught you all the manners you'd need with that high cotton, piece of crap, Chad, even though they're the ones who should have been bending over backwards to make *you* feel comfortable."

"I know, Ro. Where are you going with all of this?" I asked.

"I taught you everything I know, but I forgot to teach you how to fight."

"I don't understand—

She interrupted. "Look at me," she commanded, her gaze scoring into mine. "You. Did. Nothing. Wrong."

Tears welled up in my eyes.

"Say it," she gently commanded.

I rolled my eyes. "C'mon now," I said, trying to pull away.

But she wouldn't let go.

"Say it, Alice."

She was dead serious. I wasn't going anywhere until I did what she asked.

"You're not going to sit on my chest and dangle a spit ball over my mouth until I do what you say, are you?" She used to do that when we were kids.

I was going for levity. She responded with determined stoicism.

I let out a frustrated sigh, looked her in the eye, and I said it, "I did nothing wrong."

She nodded. "Again."

I swallowed. "I did nothing wrong."

"I almost believe you," she said, a hint of a smile coming up. "Again."

I took a deep breath and let it out.

I am so tired of being afraid.

"I did *nothing* wrong," I said, actually starting to feel it.

They took my photo without my consent. I'm not letting them take anything else from me.

"There she is," she whispered. "One more time."

"I. Did. Nothing. Wrong."

"That's my girl," she said, letting out a deep sigh. "Now you're ready."

She was right.

I *was* ready.

I was also lonely, missing City more than I expected. I could keep busy all day, but as soon as my world got quiet, as I drifted off to sleep, that's when it hit me everytime: Letting him go was a big mistake, maybe the biggest I've ever made. And I didn't know if I could fix it.

Twenty-Three

"Have I gone mad?" Alice asked.
"I'm afraid so, but let me tell you something, the best people usually are."
~Lewis Carroll, *Alice in Wonderland*

Alice

"I THOUGHT YOU said this was supposed to be a small, informal hearing?" Lulu asked.

Rayna tsk'd while looking around. "Yeah, there's nothing small or casual about any of this. It looks like you've got the whole school here."

"No, this can't be for me," I said. "Maybe there's a rally going on today, although it looks like it's about to rain cats and dogs any second now. Not a good day for a protest."

I didn't blame them for being confused. I perused the printed-out email from my advisor. She had outlined how everything was to proceed.

"It says here there are four members on the university's ethics committee, along with the dean of my department. Each gets a vote," I said. "I don't understand where all these people came from."

I was there with my best friends, all whom had taken the day off of work to accompany me. Rayna said she had her lawyer and the press on speed dial, in case 'heads needed to roll.'

God, I loved them so.

As I walked through the crowd, and I'm talking hundreds of people, I couldn't help but scan their faces, hoping to see his.

"I don't think he's here, honey," Caroline said.

She knew me too well.

I nodded, taking a deep breath. "I should have told him about today."

She grimaced. "Actually, I texted him the info yesterday," she said. "But he didn't respond . . . I'm so sorry."

Don't start crying. If you start, you won't stop. You can fall apart when this is all over.

"Thanks for trying," I said, giving a small smile.

Thunder rumbled over our heads, followed by lightning crackling through the sky.

"Let's hurry," I said.

Suddenly, I heard someone from the crowd cry out, "Hey, it's her! It's Alice!"

"Alice is here?"

"Make way! Make way!"

Just like Moses at the Red Sea, swarms of people parted right in front of us, making way so we could keep going.

"Go get 'em, Alice!"

"We're all behind you!"

"Tell the patriarchy to shove their double standards up their asses!"

We got to the building, walking to the top of the steps, but before I went in, I turned towards the crowd, amazed there were so many people out today. For me. Some even had picket signs.

I had no idea how they had found out what was happening, but I sure didn't want to let them down. So, I channeled one of my idols, Winston Churchill, and flashed 'V' for victory fingers.

The crowd went wild and the thunder grew louder.

Campus police ushered us inside the space, which looked just like a courtroom to me. The room was huge and the committee was already seated at the front.

I was on trial.

"So much for informal," I scoffed.

"I bet they saw all the ruckus and upped their game," my sister said.

It was standing room only, but there was a seat for me next to my advisor at a table in front of the committee. I took my seat and was grateful there was a bottle of water waiting.

"Perfect timing," she said, covering the microphone in front of us. "I already gave my statement. Now the committee will ask you some questions and you'll have a chance to read your prepared remarks. Are you ready?"

"You bet," I said—and I meant it too.

One of them banged a gavel several times, calling for order.

"It has come to the attention of this university's esteemed committee that you, Alice Elizabeth Leighton, were photographed in the midst of a lewd and lascivious act, which was published in a local newspaper earlier this month." The committee member held up the paper. "For the record, is this—in fact—*you* in the aforementioned picture?"

"Yes," I said.

What an asshole.

He held up a booklet. "Upon entering this esteemed university, did you sign our *Student Handbook?*"

"Yes, I did," I said.

He's really going to drag this out. That's fine. Bring it, grandpa.

"I see," he said, thumbing through it. "Did you happen to *read* the section on student conduct?"

"Yes, I did read it."

"Then you are aware in Section III, Article XI it states 'conduct which is disorderly, lewd, indecent, or which disturbs the peace may serve as cause for suspension or expulsion.'"

"I am aware of the policy, but I do not believe I violated it."

Another committee member piped in. "Yes, we heard from your advisor that this photograph was taken without your knowledge or your consent."

"That is correct," I said. "I would also like to say for the record during this 'informal' hearing, I object to the term 'lewd and lascivious' used to describe what was happening in the photo."

"You are engaging in sexual intercourse in the picture, aren't you, Ms. Leighton?"

"Yes, but as a graduate student of your esteemed clinical psychology and human sexuality studies department, I refuse to label a loving act between two consenting adults 'lewd and lascivious.' The lewd act occurred when a couple of jerks took our photo—without consent—and sold it for money, just because my partner happens to be a well-known member of this city's artistic community.

"One could also say this hearing today is also a lewd act, bringing a woman in front of an all-male committee to endure institutionalized 'slut shaming.' Shame on you. I did not give those men permission to photograph and sell my image and I do not give you permission to judge how I express myself in private, and since my partner owns that building and the land it occupies, the entirety of this supposed 'lewd and lascivious act' is, in fact, private, and none of your business."

Everyone behind me in the 'courtroom' stood up and cheered, a roar of applause and hollers the likes I'd never heard.

"You tell 'em Alice!"

"No more slut shaming!"

"Time's up! Time's up! Time's up!

He slammed the gavel down, just as the thunder shook everything in the building. "That's some storm outside," I said to Ms. Joan.

She laughed. "That's some storm inside."

"The committee will take a five-minute recess!"

"I didn't get to read my statement," I said.

"I think they got your message," she said while shaking her head, smiling.

All the girls rushed up.

"Oh my God, you were on fire!" Rayna said. "I got the whole thing on my phone!"

Lulu was practically hopping in place. "I cannot believe how rude they were, but wow, you sure told them!"

Then there was my sister.

She had no words.

But her pride shone bright and blinding.

And that's when I knew. I had already won.

IT TOOK US a while to get out of that room, but eventually, the university police were able to clear the people out so I could exit the building. Sheets of rain came down, making people scatter.

"Here, I brought you one," my sister said, handing me an umbrella.

"But what about you?" I asked.

She dug into her bag and, of course, there was another one.

"I'm always prepared," she winked.

I undid the snap and opened it up, but the storm was so bad, even with an umbrella, rain was coming at us in all directions.

"Alice, look up," one of them said.

"What?"

I couldn't see a thing. I walked down the steps with my umbrella in hand. The last of the crowd was running in all directions, people using newspapers and their backpacks to cover their heads.

Except for one.

He was standing in the rain.

And he was waiting for me.

I didn't care about anything else except getting to him.

I dropped the umbrella and ran as fast as I could.

He opened his arms wide and I fell into them.

All the air whooshed out of my lungs as I buried my face in his neck and let out all the misery I'd kept in over the last couple of weeks.

"Oh, there's my girl," he said into my skin, his mouth finding mine. "You were magnificent, the most incredible thing I've ever seen."

I paused. "You saw me?"

"I was in the back," he said, smiling down at me. "What? You think I'd miss a good ol' Southern smack down?"

I swallowed the lump of tears in my throat. "Dare, I am so sorry. I shut you out . . . you have no idea how much I've missed you . . . I can't believe you're here."

"I'm here. In fact, I traded in my first-class ticket for two economies."

He was quoting my new favorite movie, *The Goodbye Girl.*

"God, I love you," I blurted out. His whole body stilled. "Oh crap, is it too soon? Did I freak you out?"

His hold tightened. "You kidding? I've been in love with you since I rummaged through that bag of magic tricks you haul around."

I threw my head back and laughed. "It was the vibrator that did it, wasn't it?"

His eyes welled up as he kissed my forehead. "Dixie, it was everything. You are my Wonderland."

The End

Want to find out what happens with Alice and Dare?

Visit my website and sign up for my newsletter. I'll send you a subscribers-only epilogue!

www.HarperKincaid.com

Also, send me a note and let me know whose story you want to hear next in my Different Kind of Wonderland series.

Rayna, our Queen of Heart
Lulu, our White Rabbit
Caroline, our Favorite Big Sister

Stalk me via social media:
www.facebook.com/HarperKincaidRomance
www.instagram.com/CharmingWhenTipsy
www.twitter.com/HarperKincaid
www.pinterest.com/HarperKincaid

Other books by
HARPER KINCAID

Rule Breaker

Heart Breaker

Girl Breaker

Bind Me Before You Go

Acknowledgements

THIS IS THE book I've wanted to write for a long time and it wouldn't have happened without the help of some extraordinary people.

First off, I thank God because, well, you're the man. You've got my back and you love this dirty girl unconditionally. Thank you for all the blessings you've given me and those I love.

I would also like to thank my beta readers, Lisa Waldorf-Lee, Devon Hemsley, and Carrie Durbin. You are my magical, glittery, badass unicorns! Thank you to Rebecca Norinne for the most gorgeous cover on the planet. You got this project from minute one and I am grateful for your artistic vision and overall sassy mouth. Also thank you to Jamaila Brinkley for organizing my favorite writing retreat, which gave me the time and space to bring a grown-up Alice to life. A huge thank you to Delancey Stewart, who was editing this book until the very last minute. Your insights and guidance were invaluable and I adore you. Thanks to Jessica Estep and Kelly Simmons from InkSlingers—you two are my dream team of publicity and common sense. Thank you for listening to me rattle on.

Of course, thank you to my family, especially my girls, Hunter and Samara. You interrupted a lot, but that's okay. You're always worth it.

About the Author

BORN IN CALIFORNIA and raised in South Florida, Harper Kincaid has moved around like a gypsy with a bounty on her head ever since. For years, she was a jill of all trades and a master of none, but is now tickled hot pink to pen stories that break and mend people's hearts for a living. Ms. Kincaid believes seduction occurs from the neck up, which is why her characters are smart, sexy, and slightly quirky-definitely worthy to be your next hard-core book crush.

When not writing, she adores listening to indie, lo-fi, complaint rock played on vinyl, the theater, well-informed optimism, happy endings (both kinds), and making those close to her laugh 'til they snort. She is a self-admitted change junkie, loving new experiences and places, but has now happily settled in the cutest lil' town, Vienna, Virginia.

www.HarperKincaid.com

Made in the USA
Middletown, DE
09 February 2018